大詩人的聲音

◎成寒 編著

詩要用聽、用唸的，而不只是用「看」而已

Poetry is meant to be heard and read.

珍惜詩人的聲音

◎ 陳義芝

　　1963年詩人覃子豪逝世前，瘂弦以電台台長身分到臺大醫院病房訪問他，為詩壇保存下一卷沙啞的錄音。我沒見過覃先生，但十幾年後一個深夜，在聯副辦公室聽那卷哀傷的錄音，任長短參差的音波搔括耳膜，心頭蒼茫之感久久難去。

　　2000年隨詩人余光中等筆會成員，在莫斯科造訪托爾斯泰故居，聽留聲機播放托翁的聲音，雖不解其義，卻有在曠野向天祈禱的肅穆之感，那聲音彷彿在為貧窮農奴抗爭、為人生長苦的慾望告解。

　　作家的聲音珍貴！特別是隔代的傑出作家，他們的作品活著生命就活著，但他們的軀體已腐朽，讀者如何去親近？只有靠影像靠聲音。過去，影像保存的多，聲音相對地少，即使留聲機發明了，即使錄音設備方便至極的今天，文學聲音的出版始終不受重視。

　　2002年，傳奇詩人夏宇出了一本結合兩張CD的詩集《夏宇愈混樂隊》，讓見不到夏宇本人的夏宇迷可以聽到夏宇的聲音。2003年，作家教授廖玉蕙策劃的《繁花盛景——台灣當代文學新選》更為三十位入選的詩人、散文家、小說家留下受訪的錄音影像，具體地縮短了讀者認識作家的距離，對文學閱讀、教育、傳播都大有幫助。然而，這些，畢竟侷限在台灣，國外的詩人如何唸詩？一般人不得而知。是像「台北詩歌節」以戲劇表演為主的朗誦？是像某些誇張得使人起雞皮疙瘩的腔調？新詩可以怎麼唸，西方大詩人怎麼唸？這本《大詩人的聲音》正好滿足了我們這方面的好奇。

　　《大詩人的聲音》包含文本解說、一百多幅圖及CD錄音。由詩人原音朗誦的有葉慈、狄倫・托瑪斯、丁尼生、惠特曼、史蒂文斯、米蕾（Edna St. Vincent Milly）及葛楚・史坦（Gertrude Stein）等著名英美現代詩人。我發覺，沒有一個人破壞詩的聲調，儘管情感熾烈如江潮翻湧，但不影響吐音清晰，聽的人不必「捕風捉影」，不至於「丈二金剛摸不著頭」，清清楚楚自然沉浸詩意裡。這是我心目中最好的朗誦法。二十幾年前我在南海學園藝術教育館聽楊牧唸散文〈普林斯頓的秋天〉，聲音低沉，聽似淡漠，卻是寫〈普林斯頓的秋天〉的楊牧的聲音，輕易就把人帶入文學情境。朗誦的道理其實就在「平易近人」四個字！想要奇崛深刻，那是作品本身應具備的。因此，平庸的詩、壞詩就不適合朗誦，你再怎麼賣力也救不活它的平庸與壞。

　　這本《大詩人的聲音》選的，都是我不斷追著讀的詩人，原音朗誦的之外，由別人代讀詩句詩篇的有：莎士比亞、雪萊、濟慈、華滋華斯、布雷克、龐德、艾蜜莉‧狄瑾蓀、桑德堡………。所選的詩句、詩篇，也全是經典。試問：可以不知道莎翁的"To be , or not to be"嗎？可以不知道影響過徐志摩的布雷克的"Tiger , tiger"嗎？可以不知道「冬天到了，春天還會遠嗎」？龐德的〈在地下鐵車站〉、桑德堡的〈霧〉、狄瑾蓀的〈沒有一艘船能像一本書〉也無不是文學青年必讀的詩。

我在大學課堂曾問過學生，「生命誠可貴，愛情價更高，若為自由故，兩者皆可拋」是誰的詩？學生不知匈牙利民族詩人裴多非；問「有的人活著，他已經死了；有的人死了，他還活著」是誰的詩？學生不知臧克家更不知是紀念魯迅的；問水蔭萍、林亨泰、商禽、林泠，識得的也屈指可數。這是人文教養普遍差的關係，全社會需補上這一門課。我很同意成寒說的：與其研究詩人的技巧，不如用心品嘗詩人寄託在詩中的思想和情感，「詩，先用聽的，然後再去看它」，「詩，當你每唸一遍，就能更理解一些」。當年我上博士班詩學專題研究課時，我的老師張子良就要求學生唸詩，現在我在課堂講新詩，也要學生大聲唸詩。一時看不懂的詩，多唸幾遍，會因聲音的感染、感動而讀懂它。

本書選譯的每首詩後，成寒都附了一段她的詩話，這一部分也是十分珍貴的內容。成寒對詩創作的原理掌握精確，娓娓敘述的詩人故

事，深富情趣，一一指出哪一句哪一首出自哪一部電影，對在學院教詩而迤盼使教學活潑的人，尤其有參考指引作用。作爲寫詩、讀詩、教詩的人，我鄭重推薦這一出版新猷，希望大家重視，使我們的社會成爲一個優雅有教養的社會！

2004年10月29日，於台北內湖

（本文作者爲詩人、聯合報副刊主任）

詩，無處不在

◎ 成寒

詩，無處不在。

海倫，特洛伊的海倫，有多美？我們又如何知道呢？在沒有照相技術的年代，後世的人僅能依憑詩人馬羅的詩句去揣測，去想像。

失戀的時候要讀詩——《天涯何處無芳草》，女主角娜妲麗‧華從華滋華斯的詩中有所感悟。

連蜘蛛人也讀詩——《蜘蛛人2》，為了追求心愛的女孩。

美麗的詩，感動的詩。詩人用詩的語言給我們傳遞了幽微密觸的情感，那水壺的咕嚕聲，那小提琴的啜泣，那細細的笛音……1888年，愛迪生剛發明了留聲機，特意找來當代最著名的詩人丁尼生、白朗寧，朗讀他們自己的詩，在沒有電視和廣播的時代，能夠留住這些世紀之音，讓一百多年後的我們聆聽欣賞。可惜的是，艾蜜莉‧狄瑾蓀趕不及這一場盛會，在前兩年已香消玉殞。更早以前，雪萊、濟慈、華滋華斯、布雷克，一個個也都錯過了，倘若他們能夠留下一點聲音，尤其是朗誦詩歌的聲音，將多麼令人震顫和悸動！

*　　　　*　　　　*

白朗寧朗讀之際，年紀已近八十，當他初次見到留聲機，那興奮激動的心情完全表現在他的聲音裡，朗誦完畢，他以及在場的人，竟高興得拍手叫好。雖然當時錄音的效果不太好，但仍能從老詩人的聲音中感受到詩的強烈情感。

詩人創造語言。

在這本書裡，我也要為白朗寧叫屈，為詩人翻案。

建築界人士無所不知的一句名言：「少即是多」（Less is more.）。多年來，大家都以為是二十世紀建築四大師之一，曾任德國包浩斯學院院長的密斯凡德羅（Ludwig Mies van der Rohe）所說的，而且打著「極簡主義」的口號應用在設計上，越叫越響。

但實際上，這句話是出於白朗寧的詩句。

有些詩隨著時光湮沒，有些留存下來，成了我們今天常用的成語如「一見鍾情」出自馬羅；「愛過總比沒愛好」源於丁尼生；「冬天到了，春天還會遠嗎？」是雪萊說的；「我的蠟燭兩頭燒。」則來自漂亮女詩人米蕾。

*　　　　　*　　　　　*

曾獲諾貝爾文學獎的俄籍詩人約瑟夫‧布洛茲基（Joseph Brodsky, 1940-1996）生前曾在美國哥倫比亞大學的寫作研究所任教，他上課的第一天，就規定每個學生都要背幾首詩，而且要大聲背誦。其中幾首詩很長，學生起初相當氣憤，覺得功課負荷量過大。布洛茲基在流亡期間，因為勤讀詩而學會了英文。我曾經看過一本他寫的關於威尼斯的書，行文美麗如詩，唸著唸著，每個字都像一顆顆渾亮的珍珠發光。

漸漸地，在很不情願之下，學生開始背誦在課堂上用心學到的詩，從丁尼生、葉慈、奧登、雪萊以迄濟慈、狄瑾蓀，越背越朗朗上口。到了學期末，奇妙的事發生了，他們背過的詩逐漸留在他們的血液裡，跟著他們的心一起跳動。那些詩句流暢地從他們的舌尖滑了出來，其中一個女學生驚喜地說：

　　「現在我擁有這些詩了。」（I own these poems now.）

＊　　　　＊　　　　＊

　　電影《奔騰年代》（*Seabiscuit*）中感人的一幕，在加拿大亞伯達有一戶家庭，某個夜晚，爸爸在餐桌上搬出了幾本厚厚的精裝詩集，隨即起個頭："We never know how high we are－"

　　大兒子（托比・麥奎爾飾）立刻接了下去：

We never know how high we are

Till we are asked to rise

And then if we are true to plan

Our statures touch the skies－

這是艾蜜莉・狄瑾蓀的詩。

因為有了詩，一家人的感情愈發和樂融洽。

詩是凝聚家庭的精神核心。

＊　　　　＊　　　　＊

詩,無處不在。

詩,不在於其形式。與其研究詩的形式,不如努力去體會詩中所涵蘊的意義。換句話說,與其研究詩人,為了將自己的理想、情感傳達給讀者,而運用的技巧——韻律法,不如用心鑑賞、仔細品嘗詩人寄託在詩中的思想和情感本身,且把詩與自己的生活和心靈互相印證。這樣,詩就能感動你。

愛爾蘭詩人葉慈把詩當成「縫縫拆拆」(Stitching and unstiching)的高度技巧,在〈亞當的詛咒〉(Adam's Curse)一詩裡寫道:

> 我說:「一行詩也許要耗掉我們幾小時;
> 假若看起來不像是剎那間完成的作品,
> 我們的縫縫拆拆便一文不值。」

在寫詩的過程當中,一針一線地縫合,縫了又拆,拆了又縫,但做出來的東西又要令人覺得是一氣呵成,沒有斧鑿的痕跡。這樣才算是一首好詩。

         ＊   ＊   ＊

詩,若能直接唸原文,那樣更好。

從譯文去讀詩,學到的往往是主題和意象,而難以領略節奏和韻律。舉個例子,李清照詞中:「尋尋覓覓,冷冷清清,悽悽慘慘戚戚」,一連串疊字,唸起來韻味十足,感覺一下子全上來。

然而，一旦翻譯成英文，很難找到合適的字眼去搭調。

　　本書最後附錄了兩首詩，故意不去譯它。由讀者自己從詩人口中的聲調、語氣中，試著去聽，用心去聽，用心去理解，究竟詩裡詩外，有些什麼說不出的涵意。詩，當你每唸一遍，每一次就能更理解了一些。比如狄倫‧托瑪斯高聲朗讀他自己的詩，似乎具有一種莫名的感染力；即使你尚未「看」懂，至少也「聽」懂了。

　　詩，先用聽的，然後再去看它。讀詩的樂趣，逐漸浮出水面。

　　詩是生活，詩是品味。

　　詩，無處不在。

＊請注意，詩人在朗讀他們自己的詩時，有時會不經意地更改詩句，如同即興創作，以致於所唸的詩與原詩文字略有出入。

成寒部落格：www.wretch.cc/blog/chenhen

目 次

大詩人的聲音

小星星，
一閃一閃亮晶晶
The Little Star

◆ 珍‧泰勒 Jane Taylor
CD*2

珍‧泰勒
Jane Taylor（1783-1824）

英國詩人，她寫詩、聖歌，也寫童書。〈小星星〉童詩是她和姊姊安（Ann）合寫的。

Twinkle, twinkle, little star,
How I wonder what you are.
Up above the world so high,
Like a diamond in the sky.
Twinkle, twinkle, little star,
How I wonder what you are!

一閃，一閃，小星星，
我好想知道你究竟是什麼。
高高掛在天空，
像鑽石在天空放光明。
一閃，一閃，小星星，
我好想知道你究竟是什麼！

When the blazing sun is gone,
When he nothing shines upon,
Then you show your little light,

Twinkle, twinkle, all the night.
Twinkle, twinkle, little star,
How I wonder what you are!

當烈日消逝，
沒有東西可以反映光芒，
你就顯示你的微光，
一閃，一閃，亮整晚。
一閃，一閃，小星星，
我好想知道你究竟是什麼！

Then the traveler in the dark
Thanks you for your tiny spark;
He couldn't see which way to go,
If you did not twinkle so.
Twinkle, twinkle, little star,
How I wonder what you are!

旅行者在黑夜茫茫，
感謝你微弱的光芒；
他看不見走向何方，
假若你不這樣發光。
一閃，一閃，小星星，
我好想知道你究竟是什麼！

夜，俯下身來——

　　在地球上望星空，寧靜的夜晚，星光瑩瑩，萬籟俱寂。星空無語，但仔細聆聽，又恍惚可以聽見星星的聲音。星星竊竊私語，它們在說些什麼呢？

　　多星的夜晚，小女孩指向天空，用稚嫩的聲音說：

　　「爸爸，你看，黑夜有一千隻眼睛，在眨呀眨的。」

　　爸爸開心地笑了，牽起她的小手。她細細地唱起：

　　「一閃一閃亮晶晶，滿天都是小星星，掛在天空放光明，好像天上摘下的星。一閃一閃亮晶晶……」

　　隔天，她在晨光中醒來，喚爸爸，沒有回應，原來爸爸又出國去了。年復一年，每三個月回家一趟，爸爸總是帶她去看星星。

　　因為，她是爸爸最鍾愛的女兒。

　　許多年後，小女孩長大了，這時爸爸已從國外歸來，辦了退休，不再出國了。換成小女孩，懷著夢想赴異鄉求學，她打算看遍天下所有的星星，每一個國家，每一座城市。等她回來，她要把她腳步所及的地方，把她的感想，一一與爸爸分享。

　　女孩一去多年，每當她來到一座陌生城市，仰起頭，她知道在不同的時辰，在地球不同的角落，爸爸也跟著她一起看星星。不過，一方是黑夜，一方是白晝。寂渺的樂句，車窗晃動，夜色裡微笑映現，而她唱的是 "Twinkle, twinkle, little star, / How I wonder what you are!" 那時的她，寂寞和想家的心情掉了一地。

　　誰知等她回來，爸爸已遁入空門，不再戀棧世間事。她很想跟爸爸訴說這些年來她在各地看過的星空，她很想再跟爸爸一起去看星星。

　　畢竟，他是女兒最鍾愛的爸爸。

　　可是她發現，台北市區的天空，看不到星星。而，就算有星星，爸爸也無心去看了。

一個孩童在威爾斯的聖誕節
A Child's Christmas in Wales

◆狄倫·托瑪斯 Dylan Thomas

朗誦：狄倫·托瑪斯

CD*3

狄倫·托瑪斯
Dylan Thomas（1914-1953）

英國詩人，40年代英國詩壇的盟主，擁有渾厚的聲音，曾在英國廣播公司任職，朗誦別人或自己的詩歌。39歲死於紐約。

One Christmas was so much like another,
in those years, around the sea-town corner now,
and out of all sound except the distant speaking of the
voices I sometimes hear a moment before sleep, that I
can never remember
whether it snowed for six days and six nights
when I was twelve or whether it snowed for
twelve days and twelve nights when I was
six......

那些年頭每個聖誕節一如以往，
在今天海邊小鎮的角落附近，除了睡前遠方
傳來片刻的談話聲，一無聲響，
我從來不記得是我十二歲那年雪下了六天六夜
還是我六歲那年雪下了十二天十二夜……

羊齒丘
Fern Hill

◆ 狄倫・托瑪斯 Dylan Thomas
朗誦：狄倫・托瑪斯
CD*4

Now as I was young and easy under the apple boughs
About the lilting house and happy as the grass was green,
The night above the dingle starry,
Time let me hail and climb
Golden in the heydays of his eyes,
And honoured among wagons I was prince of the apple towns
And once below a time I lordly had the trees and leaves
Trail with daisies and barley
Down the rivers of the windfall light.

此刻我年輕又飄逸，站在嫩綠的蘋果樹下，
身旁的小屋活潑輕快，我幸福美好，綠草青翠，
幽谷上的夜空星光燦爛，
時光令我歡呼雀躍，
眼中的盛世金碧輝煌，
我是蘋果鎮的王子，馬車迎送，無比的榮耀，
很久以後我自會像君王擁有群樹和綠葉，
小徑長滿雛菊和大麥，
微風沿河吹拂灑落的陽光。

And as I was green and carefree, famous among the barns

About the happy yard and singing as the farm was home,

In the sun that is young once only,

Time let me play and be

Golden in the mercy of his means,

And green and golden I was huntsman and herdsman, the calves

Sang to my horn, the foxes on the hills barked clear and cold,

And the sabbath rang slowly

In the pebbles of the holy streams.

此刻我青春無擾，聲名赫赫，四周穀倉座座，

幸福的庭院深深，我一路歡歌，農場就是家園，

在一度年輕的陽光裡，

時光讓我嬉戲，

蒙受他的恩寵金光閃耀，

我是獵手，我是牧人，年輕幸福，牛犢應著

我的號角歌唱，山中狐狸冷冷的吠聲輕脆，

聖溪的鵝卵石裡

傳來安息日緩緩的鐘聲。

All the sun long it was running, it was lovely, the hay

Fields high as the house, the tunes from the chimneys, it was air

And playing, lovely and watery

And fire green as grass.

And nightly under the simple stars

As I rode to sleep the owls were bearing the farm away,

All the moon long I heard, blessed among stables, the nightjars
Flying with the ricks, and the horses
Flashing into the dark.

明媚的陽光整天地潑灑，那麼美麗可愛，
田間的乾草高及屋脊，煙囱飄出美妙的旋律，
那是嬉戲的空氣，動人又溼潤，
火中的綠燄如草。
每到夜色降臨，稀疏的星空下，
我趕著回家入眠，貓頭鷹駝著農場而去，
姣潔的月光賜福大地，我在馬廄間聆聽歐洲夜鷹
銜起乾草飛翔，一匹匹馬
光一樣閃入黑夜。

And then to awake, and the farm, like a wanderer white
With the dew, come back, the cock on his shoulder: it was all
Shining, it was Adam and maiden,
The sky gathered again
And the sun grew round that very day.
So it must have been after the birth of the simple light
In the first, spinning place, the spellbound horses walking warm
Out of the whinnying green stable
On to the fields of praise.

隨後農場醒來，像一位浪子回歸，
身披白露，肩負雄雞，陽光普照大地，
那是亞當和夏娃，

天空再次聚攏，

那一天的太陽渾圓無邊。

所以肯定是在簡潔的光芒誕生之後，

在最初旋轉的地方，消魂的馬群

熱切地走出綠色而嘶鳴的馬廄

奔馳在美好的曠野。

And honoured among foxes and pheasants by the gay house

Under the new made clouds and happy as the heart was long,

In the sun born over and over,

I ran my heedless ways,

My wishcs raced through the house high hay

And nothing I cared, at my sky blue trades, that time allows

In all his tuneful turning so few and such morning songs

Before the children green and golden

Follow him out of grace.

快樂的小屋旁，我榮幸地置身於狐群和雉雞，

在新形成的雲層下，幸福歡暢，內心悠長，

太陽日復一日地誕生，

我狂放不羈，

我的心願穿越高及屋脊的乾草，

在藍天下勞作，無憂無慮，時光在和諧的

旋律裡轉動，竟誦唱如此寥寥幾首晨歌，

隨後散發青春活力的孩子

隨他步出優雅。

Nothing I cared, in the lamb white days, that time would take me

Up to the swallow thronged loft by the shadow of my hand,

In the moon that is always rising,

Nor that riding to sleep

I should hear him fly with the high fields

And wake to the farm forever fled from the childless land.

Oh as I was young and easy in the mercy of his means,

Time held me green and dying

Though I sang in my chains like the sea.

我無所牽掛，在羔羊般潔白的日子裡，時光

拉起我的手影，在冉冉升起的月下，

爬上棲滿燕子的閣樓，

我奔波入眠，

我該聽不見他與高高的原野一起飛翔，

也不會醒來發現農場永遠逃離了沒有孩子的土地，

哦，我蒙受他的恩寵，年輕又飄逸，

時光賜我青春與死亡

儘管我戴著鐐銬依然像大海一樣歌唱。

不要柔順地走進那美好的夜晚
Do Not Go Gentle Into That Good Night

◆ 狄倫‧托瑪斯 Dylan Thomas

朗誦：狄倫‧托瑪斯

CD*5

狄倫‧托瑪斯畫像

Do not go gentle into that good night,
Old age should burn and rave at close of day;
Rage, rage against the dying of the light.

不要柔順地走進那美好的夜晚，
在白晝終結時老人也該熱血沸騰，憤慨斥責；
為日光的消逝而忿怒，忿怒吧。

Though wise men at their end know dark is right,
Because their words had forked no lightening they
Do not go gentle into that good night.

雖然聰明人最終知曉黑暗必將來臨，
因為他們的言詞並未帶來閃電般的光明，
但他們並不柔順地走進那美好的夜晚。

Good men, the last wave by, crying how bright
Their frail deeds might have
    danced in a green bay,
Rage, rage against the dying of the light.

善人臨行時叫嚷他們脆弱的德行，
本來會在青春的海灣起舞，何等歡欣，
為日光的消逝而忿怒，忿怒吧。

Wild men who caught and
    sang the sun in flight,
And learn, too late, they grieved it on its way,
Do not go gentle into that good night.

狂人攫住太陽飛逝的瞬間盡情歌唱，
很晚才意識到他們在為
途中的落日憂傷，
他們也不柔順地走進那美好的夜晚。

Grave men, near death, who see with blinding sight
Blind eyes could blaze like meteors and be gay,
Rage, rage against the dying of the light.

嚴肅的人臨死前，兩眼昏花卻明白，
失明的眼睛仍能像流星般閃爍而歡暢，
為日光的消逝而忿怒，忿怒。

And you, my father, there on the sad height,
Curse, bless me now with your fierce tears, I pray.
Do not go gentle into that good night.
Rage, rage against the dying of the light.

而您，我的父親，在這悲哀至極的時刻，
請用忿怒的淚水詛咒我，祝福我，求求您。
不要柔順地走進那美好的夜晚；
為日光的消逝而忿怒，忿怒吧！

狄倫·托瑪斯

死亡是狄倫·托瑪斯詩中最常見的主題，在他短短39年的生命中，他寫了許多詩，筆觸卻很少不去敲叩死亡的門扉。

這首詩中「美好的夜晚」，是指死亡的象徵。

在詩人眼裡，死猶如夜晚一樣，有其美好的一面，它寧靜而神祕，沒有人知道死亡以後究竟是何情景。然而，死亡又如漆黑的夜晚一般死寂，悄然無聲，在黑暗中隱藏著殺機，詩人在這片寂靜前像他父親一樣深感茫然和無能為力。當靈魂緩緩飛出窗外飛向漆黑夜裡。黎明將至，花落夢過，他不願靜待命運的安排，他也不願讓父親就這樣被判定出局，走出生命。

所以，狄倫·托瑪斯般般懇求父親，忿怒，忿怒吧！

他的語氣哀怨地：「求求您，不要柔順地走進那美好的夜晚。」

拒絕爲死於倫敦大火中的孩子哀悼

A Refusal to Mourn the Death, by Fire, of a Child in London

◆ 狄倫・托瑪斯 Dylan Thomas

朗誦：狄倫・托瑪斯

CD*5

Never until the mankind making

Bird beast and flower

Fathering and all humbling darkness

Tells with silence the last light breaking

And the still hour

Is come of the sea tumbling in harness

直到創造人類

孕育鳥獸與鮮花的偉力

和令萬物卑順的黑暗

以沉寂相告最後的燈火即滅

直到那寂靜的時辰

從澎湃的汪洋上駕臨

And I must enter again the round
Zion of the water bead
And the synagogue of the ear of corn
Shall I let pray the shadow of a sound
Or sow my salt seed
In the least valley of sackcloth to mourn

而我必須再次走進
水珠拱穹的天國
和玉蜀黍形的猶太教堂
我才會祈求聲音的陰影
或在死蔭的幽谷間
播撒我苦澀的種子去悲慟

The majesty and burning of the child's death.
I shall not murder
The mankind of her going with a grave truth
Nor blaspheme down the stations of the breath
With any further
Elegy of innocence and youth.

孩子之死的威儀和熾烈。
我不會以一種嚴竣的真理
去屠殺與她同命相依的人類，
也不會再以
哀悼天真和青春的輓歌
去褻瀆生命的駐地。

Deep with the first dead lies London's daughter,
Robed in the long friends,
The grains beyond age, the dark veins of her mother,
Secret by the unmourning water
Of the riding Thames.
After the first death, there is no other.

倫敦的女兒與第一批死者深葬，
簇擁在友誼長存的朋友中間，
永恆的沙礫，母親深色的血脈，
她隱秘地傍伴著沒有哀戚
奔流不止的泰晤士河水。
第一次喪生後，便不會再有死亡。

狄倫・托瑪斯

成寒詩話

　　1944年間，德國納粹發動「閃電戰」（Blitz），對倫敦展開一連串的猛烈轟炸，那陣子，一入夜，所有的窗戶緊掩，所有的窗簾拉攏，倫敦變成一座黑暗之城。

　　狄倫‧托瑪斯的這首詩是為哀悼一位在德軍空襲倫敦時罹難的英國小女孩而寫。

　　詩人為這種悲慘的暴行感到無比憤怒，對悄然離去的無辜小女孩付予無限哀思。雖然詩是為了表達他的悲痛，然而他卻偏偏說拒絕哀悼，他的悲痛之心只能透過詩句的暗示表現出來。他的拒絕哀悼，實際上卻是負載沉重之情的悼亡詩。

一葉草融入草坪
才能長存

◆ 狄倫・托瑪斯 Dylan Thomas
朗誦：狄倫・托瑪斯
CD*6

A blade of grass longs with the meadow,
A stonc lies lost and locked in the lark-high hill.

一葉草融入草坪才能長存，
一粒石禁閉在雲雀的山崗會迷失自己。

狄倫・托瑪斯

他的一生就是一則傳奇，詩人熱情好客，與朋友把酒盡歡。他愛交友，朋友讓他發光。他認為，光是一葉草是無法在荒原上生存的，所以他寫下這首〈進入她躺著的頭顱〉（Into her lying down head）。

　　狄倫‧托瑪斯的生命很短暫，只有39年。他天性浪漫，多情男子，而無所節制的日子卻暗藏不幸的種子。假若他能夠少喝點酒，少與人交際應酬，收斂一下放縱的生活，習慣於一人獨處，那也許他可以活得久一些，多寫一些詩。然而，如果詩人嚴肅度日，遠離人氣，那他恐怕就不再是詩人狄倫‧托瑪斯，也寫不出狄倫‧托瑪斯的詩句了。

大詩人的聲音

成寒詩話

要活，還是不要活，
這才是問題

◆ 莎士比亞 William Shakespeare

CD*6

莎士比亞
William Shakespeare
（1564-1616）

英國詩人、劇作家，出生
於史特拉福，十三、四歲
時，家道中落，他只好輟
學，做過多種行業，後來
參加劇團，展開舞台和創
作生涯。他寫了兩首長詩
《維納斯與阿童尼》、《魯
克麗絲受辱記》，154首
《十四行詩》以及多齣戲
劇。

To be, or not to be: that is the question.

要活，還是不要活，這才是問題。

莎士比亞的這句話經常被引用，可是說的人往往不解其意。

《哈姆雷特》（*Hamlet*）是莎士比亞四大悲劇之一。一個人的性格就注定了他的命運，莎士比亞的悲劇就是性格的悲劇。

這齣戲的男主角是丹麥王子哈姆雷特，他天生優柔寡斷，性格明顯的延宕遲疑。當他對活在世上產生疑惑時，死的念頭也隨之而生，可他又對該不該死有了疑問。他的獨白：

「要活，還是不要活，這才是問題。」（To be, or not to be: that is the question.）

起初，哈姆雷特覺得：死，不管是心痛皮痛肉痛，死，就是睡眠，正好一了百了。

然後，他的性格又開始自我折磨：死，就是睡眠，而睡眠也許要做夢，這就麻煩了！他想到死後也不得安寧，活著已是痛苦，死後又不知會有什麼苦難？唉，To be or not to be，真是兩難啊！

她愛我，她不愛我

◆ 雪萊 Percy Bysshe Shelley
CD*6

雪萊
Percy Bysshe Shelley
（1792-1822）

英國浪漫主義詩人。
1811年，因發表《無神
論的必然性》而遭牛津
大學開除，後流亡義大
利，在海邊航船，不幸
遇難。他的妻子瑪麗‧
雪萊（Mary Shelly）著
有《科學怪人》一書。

She loves me——loves me not.

她愛我——她不愛我。

你說：愛情不是一道摘花瓣的習題。可是，為什麼還是有許多人跑去算命，看星座或拿花朵來卜卦呢？

翻閱德國大文豪歌德1808年的著作，《浮士德》第一部，其中有一段如此寫道：

瑪格麗特摘取一朵星花，把花瓣片片剝下，口中唸唸有詞。

浮士德問她：「妳在唸些什麼？」

瑪格麗特不理他，繼續剝著花，每剝下一片就說：「他愛我──」然後又剝下第二片、第三片：「他不愛我──他愛我──」直到剝下最後一片，她欣喜的喊：「他愛我！」

不知當年歐洲的詩人之間是否時相往來，或者起碼讀過別人的作品。歌德之後，約莫過了十多年，英國出現一個年輕詩人雪萊，他在1821年〈致愛德華‧威廉斯〉（To Edward Williams）的詩中，也引用類似的詩句：

Full half an hour, to-day, I tried my lot
With various flowers, and every one still said,
'She loves me-loves me not.'

今天有整整半個小時，我用各種花朵
算命，每朵花依舊說：
「她愛我──她不愛我。」

當愛情仍是曖昧不明時，心中有所疑惑，有的人徬徨無主，失了神；有的人跑去算命，也有的好像把她的愛情命運全交給了花兒。

馬修‧麥康納（Matthew McConaughey）和凱特‧哈德森（Kate Hudson）主演的電影《絕妙冤家》（How to Lose A Guy in 10 Days?），在戲的結尾時，男主角仍弄不清女主角的心意。他的同事欲知究竟，便問他："She loves you, she loves you not."

究竟，他（她）愛不愛你呢？數一數，看有多少花瓣？讓花兒告訴你答案。

冬天到了，
春天還會遠嗎？

◆雪萊 Percy Bysshe Shelley

CD*6

If Winter comes, can Spring be far behind?

冬天到了，春天還會遠嗎？

成寒詩話

這句詩出自〈西風頌〉（Ode to the West Wind）。

雪萊（1792-1822）唸牛津大學時，因發表〈無神論的必然性〉，在1811年遭學校開除。此後，他赴愛爾蘭參加民族解放運動，已婚的他，又迷戀上後來寫《科學怪人》（Frankenstein）的瑪麗。他的無神論、激進的行為及不道德的緋聞，受到當時社會的譴責，只好流亡義大利，1822年在海上遇難。

雪萊寫《西風頌》期間，正經歷一場人生危機，精神狀態處於絕望的邊緣，在這種情況下，他求助於西風，祈求西風賜予他強大的力量。

從季節的交替更迭，詩人看到了希望。一年的死亡也預示著一年的新生，在詩的最後二行，他有感而發：「啊，西風，如果冬天到了，春天還會遠嗎？」希望也就隨之而來。

老母親之歌
The Song of the Old Mother

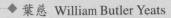

◆ 葉慈 William Butler Yeats

朗誦者：葉慈

CD*7

葉慈
William Butler Yeats
（1865-1939）

愛爾蘭詩人。出生於都
柏林，幼年曾隨律師父
親長居倫敦十多年，
1923年榮獲諾貝爾文學
獎。

I rise in the dawn, and I kneel and blow
Till the seed of the fire flicker and glow.
And then I must scrub, and bake, and sweep,
Till stars are beginning to blink and peep;
But the young lie long and dream in their bed
Of the matching of ribbons, for bosom and head,
And their day goes over in idleness,
And they sigh if the wind but lift up a tress.
While I must work, because I am old
And the seed of the fire gets feeble and cold.

我黎明即起，跪地吹火
直到爐火中火種熠熠閃爍；
然後做飯擦地清掃房間
直到晚星開始眨眼偷看；
年輕女孩在床上久睡夢想
胸飾和頭飾是否正恰當，
她們的日子逍遙又安逸，
風吹髮絲她們也要嘆息：
而我得勞作因為我老了，
火種已變得微弱冰涼了。

N° 10

30

一股寂寞的愉快衝動

◆ 葉慈 William Butler Yeats

CD*8

A lonely impulse of delight.

一股寂寞的愉快衝動。

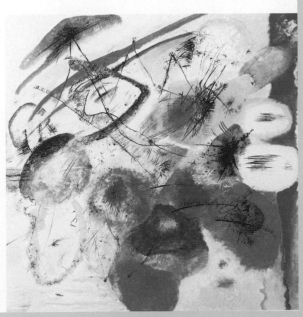

一位年輕動物學家，在什麼樣的動機下，他竟會想去教猩猩開口說話？

在《剛果》(*Congo*)這部電影中，艾美是一隻七歲大的猩猩，在剛果被捕獲後，轉賣給美國一所大學作研究用途。由該校靈長類動物學家艾略特博士負責照管這隻猩猩。後來，他開始教猩猩說話。女主角感到好奇，便問他：

「你怎麼會想到教猩猩說話？」

「一股寂寞的愉快衝動下。」（A lonely impulse of delight.）

這句簡短而漂亮的英語，出自愛爾蘭詩人葉慈（William Butler Yeats, 1865-1939）的詩〈一個愛爾蘭飛行員預見死亡〉（An Irish Airman foresees his Death），這首詩僅短短16行，是葉慈為他的女性至交——萬列格里夫人的兒子而寫。

萬列格里夫人的獨子羅伯‧葛列格里（Robert Gregory）在一次大戰中擔任飛行員，他知道此趟出任務可能會死亡，但他依然要去。他既不恨對方（敵人），也不喜歡己方（保護的人民）；他打戰沒有任何政治或道德上的原因。羅勃‧葛列格里1918年在義大利空中墜亡，葉慈先後寫了四首詩哀悼死者。

Nor Law, nor duty bade me fight,
Nor public men, nor cheering crowds.
A lonely impulse of delight.

沒有法律義務規定我去打，
也沒有大人物和群眾歡呼送行，
一股寂寞的愉快衝動。

是的，有些人做有些事，有時候是沒有任何理由的，他們想做，只是因為剛好有這個契機，出於「一股寂寞的愉快衝動」，然後就去做了。沒有人規定他，也沒人強迫他，這樣做的結果，有時還比精心策畫者做得更好。

有個老美朋友問我，為何近年來寫了多本各類不同的書？我攤開手，一笑，回答他：

"A lonely impulse of delight."

對方立刻明白了。因為，有些事是說不上來的，然而一句短短的詩，就能說明白。再多的原因或理由，都是多餘的。

庫爾莊園和峇里麗
Coole and Ballylee, 1931

◆ 葉慈 William Butler Yeats

朗誦：葉慈

CD*8（自第3、4段，打*處）

Under my window-ledge the waters race,
Otters below and moor-hens on the top,
Run for a mile undimmed in Heaven's face
Then darkening through 'dark' Raftery's 'cellar' drop,
Run underground, rise in a rocky place
In Coole demesne, and there to finish up
Spread to a lake and drop into a hole.
What's water but the generated soul?

在我的窗台下面那河水湍急奔流，
水獺在水底下游，水雞在水面上跑，
在上天的俯瞰下清亮亮地流過一哩路
然後漸漸黑暗落入「黑暗的」拉夫特瑞的「地窖」，
鑽入地下，在庫爾莊園的一塊岩石裸露的
地方升起，在那裡舒展到一個湖泊裡，
墜落到一個洞穴裡才算終結。
水不是繁衍孳生的靈魂又是什麼？

Upon the border of that lake's a wood
Now all dry sticks under a wintry sun,
And in a copse of beeches there I stood,

For Nature's pulled her tragic buskin on
And all the rant's a mirror of my mood:
At sudden thunder of the mounting swan
I turned about and looked where branches break
The glittering reaches of the flooded lake.

在那湖泊的岸邊上有一片樹林子，
此時在冬季的太陽下面全是乾枯的枝條，
在那裡的一小片櫸樹林裡我曾經佇立，
因為自然女神上演了她的悲劇，
那所有的怒吼都是我的心境的鏡子：
聽見天鵝起飛的驟然的雷霆巨聲，
我轉過身去看樹枝在何處擊破
那泛濫的湖泊的粼粼閃耀的水波。

*Another emblem there! That stormy white
But seems a concentration of the sky;
And, like the soul, it sails into the sight
And in the morning's gone, no man knows why;
And is so lovely that it sets to right
What knowledge or its lack had set awry,
So arrogantly pure, a child might think
It can be murdered with a spot of ink.

那裡還有另一個標誌！那風暴的白色
就好像是天空的凝聚濃縮；
像靈魂一樣，它飄入人們的視野，
在清晨卻消逝了，沒有人知道為什麼；

而又那麼美好：它改正了
知識或知識的匱乏所犯下的過錯，
那麼傲然純淨，一個孩子也許會想
那可以用一點墨跡毀壞弄髒。

*Sound of a stick upon the floor, a sound
From somebody that toils from chair to chair;
Beloved books that famous hands have bound,
Old marble heads, old pictures everywhere;
Great rooms where travelled men and children found
Content or joy; a last inheritor
Where none has reigned that lacked a name and fame
Or out of folly into folly came.

一根手杖戳在地板上的聲音，一種
來自某個從椅子到椅子辛勞的人的聲音；
著名的手裝訂過的可愛的書牆，
古老的石雕頭像，古老的繪面到處都是；
旅行的人們和孩子們在其中覺得滿意
和愉悅的大房間；一位最後的繼承人
在那不曾有過一個缺乏名望
或不斷幹蠢事者統治過的地方。

A spot whereon the founders lived and died
Seemed once more dear than life; ancestral trees,
Or gardens rich in memory glorified
Marriages, alliances and families,
And every bride's ambition satisfied.
Where fashion or mere fantasy decrees

葉
慈

Man shifts about——all that great glory spent——
Like some poor Arab tribesman and his tent.

一塊創建者們在上面生活和死去的地面
曾經顯得比生命更貴重；祖傳的富有
紀念意義的樹林或花園
使婚禮、姻親和家人增色添彩
每一位新娘都意足心滿。
在時尚或僅僅奇想發號施令的地方，
人四處挪動——那一切偉大榮耀都被耗盡——
就像某個貧窮的阿拉伯游牧人和他的帳篷。

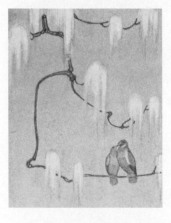

We were the last romantics——chose for theme
Traditional sanctity and loveliness;
Whatever's written in what poets name
The book of the people; whatever most can bless
The mind of man or elevate a rhyme;
But all is changed, that high horse riderless,
Though mounted in that saddle Homer rode
Where the swan drifts upon a darkening flood.

我們是最後的浪漫信徒，
挑選傳統的莊嚴和美麗當主題；
舉凡那些書寫在詩人命名稱呼
人民之書；舉凡那些極能護佑
人類之心靈或提升一韻文者。
然而一切都變了，良駿而無騎士，
縱使背上安置了當年荷馬馳騁的馬鞍
那裡天鵝漂浮在逐漸暗下來的洪水之上。

附注： 此詩作於1931年2月。

詩第一至七行，葉慈錯誤地暗示那條流經峇里鄺塔的小河流入庫爾湖。愛爾蘭詩人拉夫特瑞（1784-1835）是盲人，故說他是「黑暗的」；他有詩句：「峇里鄺塔裡的地窖堅固結實」，據說是指峇里鄺塔附近河流中的巨大深穴。

葛列格里夫人在金錢上支持他，在精神上鼓舞他，1909年，葉慈獲悉她病危時，在日記中寫道：

「她一直是我的母親、朋友、姊妹、兄弟。」

葛列格里夫人28歲時嫁給63歲的威廉·葛列格里爵士，在高爾威（Galway）郡擁有一座庫爾莊園。1892年，丈夫過世後，她提供庫爾莊園作為文學家和藝術家中心，自1897年起，葉慈每一年夏天都在那兒渡過，連續20年。這是理想的工作環境，他的許多詩，意象靈感都得自於庫爾莊園的生活體驗。

1917年葉慈在好友葛列格里夫人的兒子羅勃·葛列格里的聳恿下，買下離庫爾莊園不遠的峇里鄜塔（Thoor Ballylee），Thoor即愛爾蘭語「塔」，一座諾曼式塔樓。經過整修，從1922年至1929年，葉慈和家人在此度過夏天。

這是詩人第一次擁有自己的房子。塔樓為石板所砌，樓高四層，以迴旋梯盤旋而上，共72階。詩人對幽居「孤寂之塔」追求智慧的景況有所憧憬，他寫了一首詩獻給妻子：

> 我，詩人威廉·巴特勒·葉慈
> 以古老的石塊和海綠石板
> 戈特打鐵鋪鑄造的材料
> 為我妻子喬治重修此塔；
> 當一切再度淪為廢墟，
> 但願這些文字留存下去。

朋友來作客，依傍著古塔中的泥炭爐火共進晚餐，他如此寫道：「談話已經到了深夜時辰，爬上狹窄的迴旋梯去就寢。」

詩人在塔中，塔也在詩人心中。

因庫爾莊園和峇里鄜塔而得靈感，葉慈寫下詩集《庫爾的野天鵝》（*The Wild Swan at Coole*, 1919），在1923年榮獲諾貝爾獎之後，他又寫下《塔》（*The Tower*, 1928）、《迴旋梯詩集》（*The Winding Stair and Other Poems*, 1933）。

當你老了
When You Are Old

◆葉慈 William Butler Yeats

CD*9

年輕時代的葉慈。

葉慈

When you are old and grey and full of sleep,
And nodding by the fire, take down this book,
And slowly read, and dream of the soft look
Your eyes had once, and of their shadows deep;

當你老了，頭白了，睡意沉沉，
爐火旁打盹，請取下這部詩集，
慢慢讀，回想你過去柔和的眼神，
回想它們往昔濃重的陰影；

How many loved your moments of glad grace,
And loved your beauty with love false or true,
But one man loved the pilgrim Soul in you,
And loved the sorrows of your changing face;

多少人愛你歡喜優雅的時辰，
以假意或眞心愛你的美貌，
唯有一個人愛你朝聖的靈魂，
愛你變化面容的憂愁；

And bending down beside the glowing bars,
Murmur, a little sadly, how Love fled
And paced upon the mountains overhead
And hid his face amid a crowd of stars.

垂下頭來，在紅光閃耀的爐子旁，
有些淒然地，低低訴說那愛情的消逝，
在頭頂的山上緩緩踱著步子，
在一群星星中間隱藏著臉龐。

葉慈終生愛戀的女人
—茉德‧岡

葉慈

這首詩寫於1892年，葉慈爲茉德・岡（Maud Gonne）而作。

1889年，葉慈23歲，在異鄉倫敦初識茉德，一見面便驚爲天人，他在《回憶錄》中寫道：「我從沒想到會在一個活生生的女子身上看到如此這般的美麗。」見面的那一刻，注定了他大半輩子的苦戀與折磨。

茉德是詩人終生戀慕的對象。她是美麗動人的女演員，亦是激烈的革命份子，是愛爾蘭民族自治運動的領導人之一。詩人長期傾慕，卻追求不得，相思成爲他作詩源源不絕靈感的來源。在詩中，葉慈把茉德・岡積極追求愛爾蘭獨立的運動視爲一種「朝聖」。

這首詩暗示著歲月的無情，青春易逝，那些追求你的人只不過愛你的美貌，唯有「一個人」即詩人自己，才愛你「朝聖」的靈魂。等你年老色衰，情人也許就離你而去。唯有我愛你不渝，即使你已老去。

葉慈的許多詩，全是爲了茉德而寫。而茉德一而再拒絕葉慈的求婚，令他的苦戀始終找不到出口。正因爲茉德是葉慈「失去的女人」，她於是成爲他想像中最縈念的對象，而他又把這難解的相思化爲文，化爲詩，化爲不朽的藝術創作。若不是爲了向她傾訴情意，葉慈很可能不寫詩也說不定。他爲她寫了至少一百首以上的詩。難怪茉德・岡一度對詩人說：「世人應該感謝我沒嫁給你。」

長腳蠅
Long-legged Fly

◆ 葉慈 William Butler Yeats
朗讀：狄倫‧托瑪斯
CD*10

That civilisation may not sink,
Its great battle lost,
Quiet the dog, tether the pony
To a distant post;
Our master Caesar is in the tent
Where the maps are spread,
His eyes fixed upon nothing,
A hand under his head.

Like a long-legged fly upon the stream
His mind moves upon silence.

為使文明不沉淪，
偉大戰役不打輸，
叫狗安靜，把小馬
在遠處的木樁栓好；
我們的主人凱撒帳幕中，
地圖在面前攤開，
他雙目無所專注，
一隻手支著腦袋。

像長腳蠅飛越水面，
他腦子沉寂中運轉。

That the topless towers be burnt
And men recall that face,
Move most gently if move you must
In this lonely place.
She thinks, part woman, three parts a child,
That nobody looks; her feet
Practise a tinker shuffle
Picked up on a street.

爲把無頂塔燒掉，
讓人們追念那臉龐
輕輕走動，如有需要
在這孤寂的地方。
她以爲沒有人瞧見
小牛是婦人，大牛是孩子
她跳起笨拙的曳步舞，
從街頭學來的。

Like a long-legged fly upon the stream
Her mind moves upon silence.

像長腳蠅飛越水面，
她腦子沉寂中運轉。

That girls at puberty may find
The first Adam in their thought,
Shut the door of the Pope's chapel,
Keep those children out.
There on that scaffolding reclines

Michael Angelo.
With no more sound than the mice make
His hand moves to and fro.

為使懷春女思念中
見到第一個亞當，
把教堂大門關上，
不讓孩子們進來。
　　　米開朗基羅
仰躺在那鷹架上。

彷如老鼠無聲爬過，
　　他的手移下移上。

Like a long-legged fly upon the stream
His mind moves upon silence.

像長腳蠅飛越水面，
　　他腦子沉寂中運轉。

葉慈

成寒詩話

　　本詩的三節分別敘述影響歐洲文化的三個人物。

　　第一段是凱撒大帝，正在部署如何打贏一場「為使文明不沉淪」的偉大戰役。

　　第二段「讓人們追念那臉龐」，指古希臘美人海倫，傳說她棄夫私奔，引起了特洛伊戰爭及著名的木馬屠城記。

　　第三段「他的手移下移上」，指米開朗基羅在羅馬西斯汀教堂中仰繪天花板。他畫的是〈創世紀〉的故事，畫面上，上帝賦予亞當生命，而後世的懷春少女，看到亞當的形象，心中將激起對男性的嚮往。

　　這三個人物，當他們面臨重大抉擇時，他們的思想必須超越時空，有如「長腳蠅飛越水面」在他們的「腦子沉寂中運轉」。

茵尼斯弗里湖島
The Lake Isle of Innisfree

◆ 葉慈 William Butler Yeats

朗誦：葉慈

CD*11

葉慈

I will arise and go now, and go to Innisfree,
And a small cabin build there, of clay and wattles made;
Nine bean rows will I have there, a hive for the honey bee,
And live alone in the bee-loud glade.

我就要起身前去，去茵尼斯弗里，
用泥土夾木條，在那裡築起一間小屋；
我要種下九畦豆莢，養一窩蜂來釀蜜，
在蜂聲嗡嗡的林間空地幽居獨處。

And I shall have some peace there, for peace comes dropping slow,
Dropping from the veils of the morning to where the cricket sings;
There midnight's all a glimmer, and noon a purple glow,
And evening full of the linnet's wings.

葉慈

於是我有了一些寧靜，那裡寧靜緩緩滴零，
　　墜自晨靄向蟋蟀唧唧的地方；
那裡子夜是一片燦爛，正午紫光一團，
　　傍晚紅雀無數翅膀翻飛。

I will arise and go now, for always night and day
I hear lake water lapping with low sounds by the shore;
While I stand on the roadway, or on the pavements gray,
I hear it in the deep heart's core.

我將起身前去，因為黑夜白日，
我總是聽見湖水輕舐岸邊的幽音；
我在通衢駐足，或踏著灰色石板路，
我總是聽見水聲響在心的底處。

葉慈

這首詩的詩眼在於「寧靜」二字。

　　寧靜緩緩滴零，對寧靜的渴求即是詩的主題。

　　〈茵尼斯弗里湖島〉一詩，最初發表於1890年。詩的靈感起於異鄉。一天，詩人懷著濃濃的鄉愁走在倫敦的街頭，忽聽水聲叮咚，抬眼只見一家店舖櫥窗裡安置一座小小的噴泉。此情此景令他驀然憶起愛爾蘭家鄉的湖水，於是寫下這首詩。

　　然而，詩人未曾去過茵尼斯弗里湖島，這是他想像中的永恆之境。他在詩裡描繪了安憩之鄉，但回到現實，夢中的水聲卻從此長留，響在心的底處。

　　2005年奧斯卡金像獎大贏家《登峰造擊》（Million Dollar Baby），包括最佳影片、最佳導演、最佳女主角、最佳男配角四項大獎。片中，希拉蕊史旺飾演的女拳擊手，在賽場上遭對手重擊，頸部以下全部癱瘓。在醫院治療期間，她的教練（克林伊斯威特飾）安慰她，等出院以後，到樹林中造一座小屋，讓她在那裡休養。他吟誦起葉慈的詩句：

　　　　我就要起身前去，去茵尼斯弗里，
　　　　用泥土夾木條，在那裡築起一間小屋。

在地下鐵車站
In a Station of the Metro

◆ 龐德 Ezra Pound

CD*12

龐德
Ezra Pound（1885-1972）

美國詩人及評論家。出生於
賓州，1908年前往歐洲長
居，受他影響、協助及提攜
的作家和詩人，不計其數。
二次大戰期間，他誤信墨索
里尼之言，在義大利電台攻
擊美國及羅斯福總統，以叛
國罪被捕，遣送回國。釋放
之後，返回義大利終老。

The apparition of these faces in the crowd:
Petals on a wet, black bough.

人群中這些面孔的閃現：
像溼黑的枝幹上，花瓣點點。

每當我來到一座城市，陌生的城市。穿梭於大街小巷，跳躍於站與站之間，我坐在古老的地鐵裡，所有的記憶總是不由然融入龐德的詩句裡。

地下鐵月台上等待的乘客，一張張有些模糊晃動的臉孔，一如枝幹上濕漉漉的花瓣。當列車從漆黑的隧道裡鑽出，乘客搭著電扶梯上來，來到所想念的人面前。

美國詩人龐德（1885-1972）深受東方詩歌的影響，曾為自己在中國和日本古詩中的發現欣喜萬分。他在這些詩中找到完美的含蓄、精煉的字句和淡泊的「意象」（Imagery），並運用在他的詩作中。〈在地下鐵車站〉（In a Station of the Metro）是意象詩極為著名的一首。

龐德回憶說，〈在地下鐵車站〉這個小小的鏡頭是偶然在"Metro"（巴黎地下鐵的通稱）裡得到靈感。巴黎地鐵裡人來人往，龐德將人群‧一張張模糊的臉孔比喻成雨後濕漉漉的花瓣；而黑色枝幹上猶沾著雨露的花瓣，也成了朦朧眼中的眾生群像。

花瓣與臉孔，在腦海中產生相疊的意象，令激動的他提筆寫下一首31行的詩，但他覺得表現仍不夠凝鍊，就隨手撕掉了。半年之後，他又寫了一首15行的詩，還是不太滿意。又過了一年，時間的沉澱，他把這「意象」濃縮為兩行，自認為已達到了他所期望的詩境界：在詠詩的同時，腦海中自然會浮現出當夜景色和作者的心境。

這短短的兩行詩，彷若一幅畫，代替了千言萬語。

霧

◆卡爾・桑德堡 Carl Sandburg
CD*13

桑德堡
桑德堡 Carl Sandburg
（1878-1967）

美國詩人。未受完整的
教育的他，在19歲以
前，做過各式各樣的工
作：理髮店打雜、戲院
換布景工人、運貨車工
頭、陶瓷廠學徒、洗碟
子工人、收割麥田工
人，這些生活體驗使他
贏得「工業美國的桂冠
詩人」之稱。

The fog comes
on little cat feet.

霧來了
踩著小貓的腳步

成寒詩話

這句詩出自：〈霧〉（Fog）。

　　桑德堡寫了許多詩描繪城市——芝加哥。它的詩內容充滿現代化，而詩的形式以自由化表現。他的詩沒有押韻，無傳統音節，分行，分段；詩的節奏是一種經過煉萃的現代口語腔調。

　　在這首詩裡，詩人在瀰漫著靜謐的情調中穿插了動感。「霧來了」，淡淡一筆，它的腳步宛如貓咪一樣，靜默無聲。詩中的霧是如此輕柔，它悄悄地來臨，它輕輕地移動，籠罩著城市的大街小巷，一切彷彿發生在夢中，一無聲響。

西礁島的秩序意念
The Idea of Order at Key West

史蒂文斯
Wallace Stevens
（1879-1955）

美國詩人。畢業於哈佛大學和紐約大學法學院，先做律師，後在康乃迪克州哈特福的保險公司工作，做到副總經理。他視寫作爲興趣，很少與詩壇往來。

◆ 華勒斯・史蒂文斯 Wallace Stevens
朗誦：華勒斯・史蒂文斯
CD*14

She sang beyond the genius of the sea.
The water never formed to mind or voice,
Like a body wholly body, fluttering
Its empty sleeves; and yet its mimic motion
Made constant cry, caused constantly a cry,
That was not ours although we understood,
Inhuman, of the veritable ocean.

她的歌唱超越了大海之靈。
海水從不在腦際或聲音裡成形，
像身體之爲身體，飄動著
虛袖；可它摹擬的動作
時刻在呼叫，無時無刻不引起呼叫，
雖然叫人聽懂，卻不屬於我們，
不是人類的，是眞實的海洋之音。

The sea was not a mask. No more was she.
The song and water were not medleyed sound

華勒斯・史蒂文斯

Even if what she sang was what she heard,

Since what she sang was uttered word by word.

It may be that in all her phrases stirred

The grinding water and the gasping wind;

But it was she and not the sea we heard.

大海不是一個面具，她也不是。

歌曲和水聲並非駁雜無章

即使她聽到甚麼唱甚麼，

因為她一字一句唱出口。

也許字裡行間翻動著

滾轉的水和呼嘯的風：

入耳的可是她的歌，不是海濤。

For she was the maker of the song she sang.

The ever-hooded, tragic-gestured sea

Was merely a place by which she walked to sing.

Whose spirit is this? we said, because we knew

It was the spirit that we sought and knew

That we should ask this often as she sang.

她唱的歌曲是她創造的。

蒙頭遮臉、呼天搶地的海洋

只是她沿岸漫步低唱的地方。

這是誰的神靈？深知那是

我們追尋的神靈才有此一問，

她一邊唱，還得以此一再相問。

If it was only the dark voice of the sea
That rose, or even colored by many waves;
If it was only the outer voice of sky
And cloud, of the sunken coral water-walled,
However clear, it would have been deep air,
The heaving speech of air, a summer sound
Repeated in a summer without end
And sound alone. But it was more than that,
More even than her voice, and ours, among
The meaningless plungings of water and the wind,
Theatrical distances, bronze shadows heaped
On high horizons, mountainous atmospheres
Of sky and sea.

假如只是大海陰沉的聲音
昇起，或是甚至給千萬波濤渲染；
假如只是沉海珊瑚給水牆圍著，
以及穹蒼白雲的天外之音，
儘管清越，也只是深沉氣流，
吁氣呼呼的風之言語，綿綿無盡的
長夏裡重複長夏的聲音，而且
只是聲音而已。可是不止這樣吧，
不止她的聲音，我們的聲音，
在海和風無聊的奔躍之間，
戲劇性的距離，青銅影子重疊於
高高的地平線，嶺色山嵐
縈繞天和海。

華勒斯・史蒂文斯

It was her voice that made
The sky acutest at its vanishing.
She measured to the hour its solitude.
She was the single artificer of the world
In which she sang. And when she sang, the sea,
Whatever self it had, became the self
That was her song, for she was the maker. Then we,
As we beheld her striding there alone,
Knew that there never was a world for her
Except the one she sang and, singing, made.

是她的聲音叫
天光消褪時顯得最鮮明,
給時日量度暗換的寂寥。
她是她歌中之境的唯一
塑造者。她歌唱的時候,海洋,
不管有我無我,變成了
她歌中之我,因爲她是創造者。於是
我們目睹她獨個兒怡然舉步,
領悟到她心中一無所有,只有
歌中之境,締造於歌唱之中。

Ramon Fernandez, tell me, if you know,
Why, when the singing ended and we turned
Toward the town, tell why the glassy lights,
The lights in the fishing boats at anchor there,

As the night descended, tilting in the air,
Mastered the night and portioned out the sea,
Fixing emblazoned zones and fiery poles,
Arranging, deepening, enchanting night.

雷蒙・弗南戴茲，你知道就告訴我吧，
　　爲甚麼，一曲既終，我們轉過身
面向城裡，告訴我爲甚麼閃爍的燈火
　　──停泊這裡的漁船上的燈火，
夜幕低垂以後，在空中傾斜──
　　雄據了黑夜，平分了海洋，
釐定了明亮的地帶和熾熱的兩極，
　　擺佈著、深化著、魅惑著黑夜。

Oh! Blessed rage for order, pale Ramon,
The maker's rage to order words of the sea,
Words of the fragrant portals, dimly-starred,
And of ourselves and of our origins,
In ghostlier demarcations, keener sounds.

可憐的雷蒙，尋求秩序天賜的狂熱啊！
　　創造者的狂熱，爲了把海的字句，
芬芳之門、星光隱約的字句排成秩序，
　　爲了給我們自己、我們的出處，
更陰深的界限，更銳利的聲音。

大詩人的聲音

我是個無名小卒！
那你呢？
I'm Nobody! Who are you?

艾蜜莉・狄瑾蓀
Emily Dickinson
（1830-1886）

美國詩人。23歲以前，
她的社交活躍，但不知
確切原因，從此深居簡
出，不與人來往，外人
對她的印象僅模糊一襲
白衣。生前她只以佚名
發表了幾首詩，死後四
年，詩集才問世。

◆ 艾蜜莉・狄瑾蓀 Emily Dickinson
CD*15

I'm Nobody! Who are you?
Are you-Nobody-Too?
Then there's a pair of us——don't tell!
They'd banish us, you know.

我是個無名小卒！那你呢？
你也是——無名小卒？
那我們倆是一對——別說出去！
他們容不下我們——你知道的！

How dreary——to be——Somebody!
How public——like a Frog——
To tell one's name——the livelong June——
To an admiring Bog!

做個名人多無聊！
像隻青蛙——到處招搖——
向一窪仰慕你的泥塘
在漫長的六月裡喧嚷你的名字。

艾蜜莉・狄瑾蓀

61

成寒詩話

在英語裡，"nobody"指「無名的小人物」，"somebody"指「有頭有臉的大人物」。

艾蜜莉·狄瑾蓀（1830-1886）的詩，短小精緻，語言淺顯生動，音韻跳躍閃爍，時而空靈，時而執著，如興來神到，筆隨即之，很口語化，像是獨白：「我啜飲過生活的芳醇／付出了什麼，告訴你吧／不多不少，整整一生……」

艾蜜莉·狄瑾蓀生前僅發表過寥寥幾首詩，從未出過名，不管她是自謙也好，或者根本沒有機會成大名。總之，她深知沒名、沒人注意、沒人理睬的況味。她像個女隱士，在她的家鄉麻州安默斯特（Amherst, Massachusetts）深居，多年不與人見面，在自己小小的隱居天地裡細細品味人生的哲理。然而在死後，她的名聲卻大噪，如果地下有知，不知她作何是想？

附注：
這首詩有另一版本：
別說出去！他們會到處張揚──你知道的！
Don't tell! they'd advertise—you know!

沒有一條船能像一本書
There is no frigate like a book

艾蜜莉・狄瑾蓀 Emily Dickinson

CD*15

To take us lands away,
Nor any coursers like a page
Of prancing poetry.
This traverse may the poorest take
Without oppress of toll;
How frugal is the chariot
That bears a human soul!

沒有一條船能像一部書，
帶我們遠離家園，
也沒有任何駿馬，
抵得上歡騰的詩篇。
這旅行最窮的人也能享受，
沒有沉重的開支負擔；
運載人類靈魂的馬車，
取費是何等低廉！

成寒詩話

艾蜜莉‧狄瑾蓀在一封信裡如此寫道：

「如果有一部書能使我讀過之後渾身發冷，而且沒有任何火能把我溫暖過來，我知道那一定是詩。如果我有一種天靈蓋被人拿掉的感覺，我知道那一定是詩。」

愛看書的人，不管貧窮或富有，他們的心靈領域遠超過天之涯、海之顛，直觸精神的最大快感。

特洛伊的海倫

◆ 馬羅 Christopher Marlowe
CD*16

馬羅
Christopher Marlowe
（1564-1593）

英國詩人及劇作家。他
與莎士比亞同年出生，
著有《浮士德博士的悲
劇故事》等劇，據傳他
因帳單爭執的緣故在酒
館遭人刺死，享年僅
29。

The face that launched a thousand ships.

一張發動千艘戰艦的臉孔。

成寒詩話

英國劇作家馬羅（Christopher Marlowe），以德國民間故事爲藍本，於1588年寫出《浮士德博士的悲劇故事》（The Tragical History of Doctor Faustus）。

亞各斯的海倫，又稱特洛伊的海倫。她是梅那雷阿斯（Menelaus）的妻子，卻讓自己被巴黎斯（Paris）帶到特洛伊，因此引發西元前十三世紀的特洛伊戰爭（Trojan War），展開十年烽火。美麗而水性楊花的海倫，在馬羅勾人心魂的詩筆下，海倫的容貌被譽爲「一張發動千艘戰艦」的臉。

若非容顏絕世，像這種禍水女人，終究只是「一張惹起千隻蒼蠅的臉孔」，平白討人嫌。

電影《叛艦喋血記》（Mutiny on the Bounty），法蘭奇・湯恩以戲謔的口吻朗誦這句詩，長官克拉克・蓋博便命令他盯著船上晃動不停的油燈看，看他是否能看到海倫的臉。那油燈晃呀晃，晃過來，晃過去，而他目不轉睛地盯著，盯著，盯久了，他就暈船了。

一見鍾情

◆馬羅 Christopher Marlowe

CD*16

Who ever loved, that loved not at first sight?

曾經戀愛過的人，哪個不是一見鍾情？

成寒詩話

這句詩即我們今天常說的：「一見鍾情」（Love at first sight）。

當愛情來臨，沒有人能夠選擇，是命運，是激情，把戀人推向彼此。是瞬間突發的熱情，讓他倆交會。

如果你是「決定」去愛某人，那就不算是真正的愛。

一見鍾情的篤定是美麗的；但愛情的變化無常，亦是帶有詭譎的美麗。

然而，一見鍾情並非必然。

你可以一見「沒」情，二見「淡情」，三見或四、五見之後才真正「有」情，也未嘗不可。要不然，一見鍾情之後，二見「厭情」，三見「薄」情，四、五見「傷」情，到後來，相見不如不見，有情還似無情。

電影《真情假愛》裡，專辦離婚案件的律師喬治‧克魯尼面對著貌美的客戶老婆，忍不住朗讀起這首詩：

Who ever loved, that loved not
at first sight?

啊！船長！我的船長
O Captain! My Captain

◆ 惠特曼 Walt Whitman
CD*17

惠特曼
Walt Whitman
（1819-1892）

美國詩人。出生於紐約
長島，曾擔任過老師、
印刷工人和記者。著有
《草葉集》。

O Captain! My Captain! our fearful trip is done;
The ship has weather'd every rack,
the prize we sought is won;
The port is near, the bells I hear,
the people all exulting.

啊，船長！我的船長！
我們險惡的航程已經終了，
我們的船安渡所有的驚濤駭浪，
我們所追求的勝利成果已經得到；
港口就在眼前，我已經聽見鐘聲，
人們歡呼喧成一片。

惠特曼

林肯遭暗殺身亡，惠特曼寫了一首輓詩——這首詩也許是現代英語文學中最偉大的輓詩——哀悼這位象徵美國民主自由的偉大總統。

這首詩〈啊！船長！我的船長〉（Oh! Captain! My Captain），以一個掌舵的「船長」（captain）來比喻林肯（Abraham Lincoln）總統，是再貼切不過的，最後一句：「他已渾身冰冷，停止呼吸」，意謂著林肯的死亡。

惠特曼的詩是所謂「自由詩」（free verse），採和口語與修辭，不拘詩行（line）及詩節（stanza）長短，不拘音步，也不押韻腳的自由形式。

電影《春風化雨》（Dead Poets Society）以一所美國高中為背景，由於一位英文老師的啟發，年輕男學生詩興湍飛，驀然爆發前所未有的創造力。男老師最喜歡的一首詩，就是惠特曼的 O Captain! My Captain! 戲至最後一幕，目送著英文老師離去，學生依依不捨，一個接一個都站到桌子上，不顧他人眼光，高聲喚著：O Captain! My Captain! O Captain! My Captain! 此起彼落，男老師怔怔佇立，眼裡噙著淚水，說不出話來。

美國
America

◆ 惠特曼 Walt Whitman
朗讀：惠特曼
（CD*18，僅唸前四句）

Centre of equal daughters, equal sons,
All, all alike endear'd, grown, ungrown, young or old,
Strong, ample, fair, enduring, capable, rich,
Perennial with the Earth, with Freedom, Law and Love,
A grand, sane, towering, seated Mother,
Chair'd in the adamant of Time.

平等的女兒、平等的兒子們的中心，
讓大家，成年和未成年的，年輕和年老的，同樣地
被珍愛簇擁在周圍，
堅強、寬厚、美好、忍耐、能幹、富裕，
與大地，與自由、法律和愛永遠在一起，
作爲一個莊嚴、明智而崇高的母親，
端坐在時間的剛玉般的交椅裡。

惠特曼

成寒詩話

惠特曼（1819-1892）是美國平民詩人。

1855年七月《草葉集》（*Leaves of Grass*）問世，全書僅90頁，收集12首無題的詩。書上沒有刊出作者的姓名，只附一張畫像，畫中人一手插腰，一手插入褲袋中，帽子斜歪，領口敞開，露出瀟灑豪放的氣慨。

《草葉集》的書名由來：在自然界裡，最平凡、最頑強、最富生命力的，就是隨處可見的青草。惠特曼於是把詩集取名《草葉集》，因為「我認為一片草葉的重要並不亞於星球的運行」（I believe a leaf of grass is no less than the journey——work of the stars.）。哪裡有土，哪裡有水，哪裡就長著青草。

可惜的是，當年讀者反應冷淡，《草葉集》初版幾乎賣不出去。

次年《草葉集》再版，收錄32首詩，每首加上標題。1860年又有第三版，詩的數目增至157首。我們今天所見的《草葉集》，共有382首詩。美國每一位小學生都讀過惠特曼的詩。

惠特曼是第一位真正的美國詩人，與英國文學脫離血緣，他的詩灌注於這塊美洲新大陸，他禮讚並擁抱美國國民，和美國渾為一體，他的詩是民主美國的現代史詩。

花開堪折直須折

◆ 羅伯特‧赫里克 Robert Herrick

CD*19

赫里克
Robert Herrick
（1591-1674）

英國詩人及神職人員。

Gather ye rosebuds while ye may,
Old Time is still a-flying:
And this same flower that smiles today
Tomorrow will be dying.

玫瑰花開堪折直須折，
時光依然飛逝，
今日芬芳的花朵，
明日或已凋萎。

從過去、現在到未來，時間恍如無情地一直流動。時間的流動，象徵著歲月的消逝。在《春風化雨》這部電影中，羅賓·威廉斯飾演一所貴族高中的英文老師，面對這群青春朝氣的年輕小伙子，他有感而發，吟出這段詩句。

　　在十六、七世紀的英國詩壇，愛情詩人總是以詩代替甜言蜜語，情意切切地懇求他們的情人，請她們在擁有青春和美貌時屈從於愛情，及時行樂，莫讓青春虛度。

　　這是十七世紀英國詩人羅伯特·赫里克一首非常著名的詩〈勸女于歸〉（To the Virgins, to Make Much of Time），或譯〈女孩，請把握時光〉，敦勸年輕女孩，青春時光不再，要好好把握。

　　而今，人們引用這句詩，不僅是指女孩而已，且延伸至所有的年輕人，如同《春風化雨》電影中，羅賓·威廉斯對他的學生所言：「把握住今天」（seize the day）。在寫作或談話時，英美人士常引用這段詩。

　　這段詩，也有人以中國古詩翻譯：「采采薔薇，及其未萎；日月其邁，韶華如飛；今夕此花，灼灼其姿；翌日何如，將作枯枝。」

　　ye：（n.）你、你們，you 的古字

　　a-flying: 古英語會在動詞或現在分詞之前加上 a-，表示一個動作正在進行。一首英國兒歌Father's gone a-hunting意思是說「爸爸去打獵了」。

羅伯特·赫里克

大
詩
人
的
聲
音

天涯何處無芳草

◆華滋華斯　William Wordsworth
CD*19

華滋華斯
William Wordsworth
（1770-1850）

英國浪漫主義詩人。長期定居湖區（Lake District），1798年與柯爾律治合作發表《抒情歌謠集》。

Though nothing can bring back the hour
Of splendour in the grass, of glory in the flower;
We will grieve not, rather find
Strength in what remains behind.

雖然任誰也無法挽回
草木欣欣向榮，花卉再放的那一刻，
我們不要去悲嘆感傷，寧可
在殘餘中找尋力量。

蘇珊今年剛過50，她是我唸大學時期的英美文學教授，研究莎翁戲劇。一回，她告訴我們：「在教書的頭十年，除了研究悲劇作品，生命中不曾遇過什麼真正的悲劇。」

言猶在耳，然而，一場火災意外發生，她的身體70％燒傷，生存機會不到20％。

蘇珊在醫院裡昏迷了整整一個月，身上打上石膏，動彈不得。我們幾個學生約了去看她。她喉嚨插了呼吸管，不能講話，整個人軟弱無助，唯有一雙眼睛迷茫轉動，像是禁錮在自己體內的囚犯。看到她的模樣，我忍不住顫慄，她的狀況超乎我想像的嚴重。

然而，歷經長達半年與死神的博鬥，她漸漸能坐了，能站了，也能自己走路了。

出院以後，我們為她辦了一場慶祝重生會。當著眾人的面，她的眼中蒙上一層淚翳，用微弱的聲音，斷斷續續地背誦了英國詩人華滋華斯的詩句：「雖然任誰也無法挽回／草木欣欣向榮，花卉再放的那一刻，／我們不要去悲嘆感傷，寧可／在殘餘中找尋力量。」我們的眼睛也濕潤了。

這是她最喜愛的一首詩，華滋華斯〈頌詩：憶幼年而悟不朽〉（Ode on Intimations Of Immortality From Recollections of Early Childhood），又譯〈不朽頌〉，這首詩曾經在人生不同的階段，給過她許多安慰。

華滋華斯

　　我對這首詩印象最深刻是在1961年伊力‧卡山（Elia Kazan）導演的電影《天涯何處無芳草》（*Splendor in the Grass*），故事發生在1928年的堪薩斯小鎮，一個美麗的高中女學生（娜妲麗‧華飾）與男友深深相愛，男孩（華倫‧比提飾）是高中美式足球隊的四分衛，出盡了風頭。在別人的眼裡，兩人是天生一對。

　　然而，受到傳統道德及雙方父母的約束，兩人不敢有更進一步的親密關係。他們如此深愛對方，有了喜悅也有恐懼，終因壓抑、誤會以及種種細故，讓兩人的感情就這樣嘎然而止，斷線了。由於自尊心受創，女孩脆弱沉淪卻無力挽救，住進了精神病院，男孩則進入耶魯大學唸書。此際，適逢美國1929年股市大崩盤，男孩的父親破產，在寂寞無助之下，男孩娶了當地餐館女侍為妻，中斷學業，返鄉務農，生了幾個小孩。而女孩的病情逐漸好轉，在醫院裡認識了一名同是病患的醫生，與他交往訂婚，生命有了新的開始。

　　幾年過去，兩人再相見，恍如隔世。

　　最初的愛戀，已然遠去。驀然間，女孩想起了當年英文老師教過他們的一首詩：「雖然任誰也無法挽回／草木欣欣向榮，花卉再放的那一刻……」短短幾句，有情有景有慨嘆。華滋華斯的詩反映了那曾經擁有的已一去不回，烘托出一種悲傷過後，重新再來的人生意境。

第一株無花果
First Fig

◆ 米蕾 Edna St. Vincent Millay

CD*19

米蕾
Edna St. Vincent Millay
（1892-1950）

美國詩人。這個貌美的女子，
愛情的不可靠，是她詩中常出
現的主題。

My candle burns at both ends;
It will not last the night;
But, ah, my foes, and, oh, my friends—
It gives a lovely light.

我的蠟燭兩頭燒；
燒不到夜盡；
然而，啊，我的仇敵，
以及，我的朋友——
它提供了美好的光。

米蕾

我不久就會忘記你，親愛的

I Shall Forget You Presently, My Dear

◆米蕾 Edna St. Vincent Millay
朗誦：米蕾
CD*20

I shall forget you presently, my dear,
So make the most of this, your little day,
Your little month, your little half a year,
Ere I forget, or die, or move away,

我不久就會忘記你，親愛的，
所以不如善用這一段時光，幾天，
幾個月，或半年光景。
在我遺忘、死亡，或搬遷之前，

And we are done forever; by and by
I shall forget you, as I said, but now,
If you entreat me with your loveliest lie
I will protest you with my favorite vow.
I would indeed that love were longer–lived,
And oaths were not so brittle as they are,

米蕾

而我們已經永遠結束了；不久
我將忘記你，如我所言，但現在，
若你用最動人的謊言懇求我
我將以最喜愛的誓言來抗議，

But so it is, and nature has contrived
To struggle on without a break thus far,——
Whether or not we find what we are seeking
Is idle, biologically speaking.

但事已如此，大自然早已計畫好
持續奮鬥不斷到如今，——
不管我們是否尋著我們所要追求的
全是虛擲，就生物界而言。

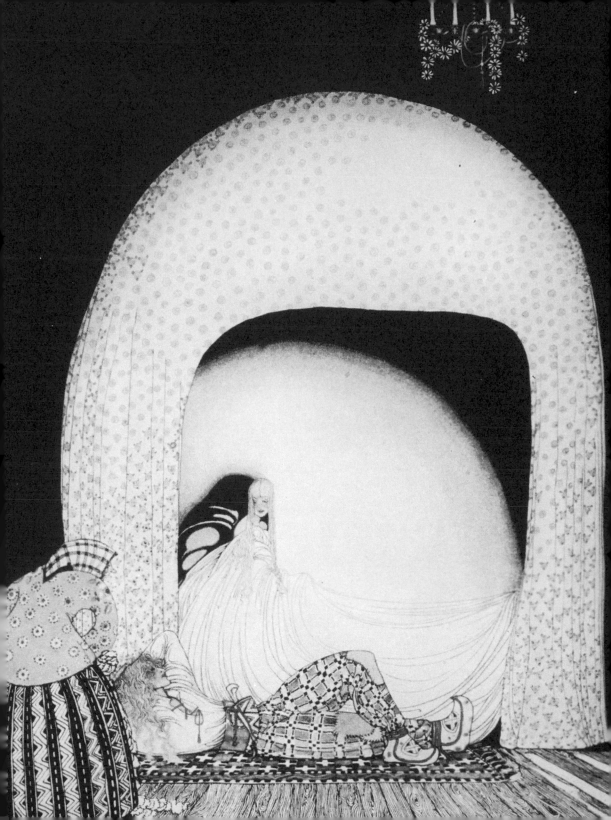

成寒詩話

「**我**不久就會忘掉你，親愛的，
所以不如善用這一段時光。」

1920年代，思想先進的美國女詩人米蕾大膽喊出男女平等的口號，強調兩性不僅在心智上無分軒輊，在生理上也應平等的說法。然而，她本身不只是個詩人，而且是貌美的女詩人，她寫出這首詩，一時之間，令她的仰慕者對其人與其詩不免有些遐想。

米蕾是普立茲獎創辦70年以來，第一位獲獎的女詩人。聽她朗讀自己的詩，彷彿有女人在唱歌。

而在〈第一株無花果〉中，「我的蠟燭兩頭燒」這句詩，曾出現在電影《蝙蝠俠：開戰時刻》，飾演女主角的凱蒂荷姆斯（湯姆克魯斯的第三任老婆）對忙碌奔波的蝙蝠俠說的。

傷心的故事
The Sad Tale

◆ 柯爾律治 Samuel Taylor Coleridge

CD*20

柯爾律治
Samuel Taylor Coleridge
（1772-1834）

英國詩人、思想家。他曾與華滋華斯合作發表詩集《抒情歌謠集》，並作一系列演講，集成《關於莎士比亞講演集》一書。

To meet, to know, to love, and then to part.
Is the sad tale of many a human heart.

相逢，相知，相慕，然後相別離，
這是許多人的傷心故事。

成寒詩話

　這首詩僅短短兩行，文字非常簡潔。所用辭彙，除兩個雙音節字外，均為單音節字。它只用四個單字：相逢（meet），相知（know），相慕（love），相別離（part），四個短短的單字，就對人生聚散的常情，予以道破。讀了這兩行詩，令人感傷。這首言淺意深的短詩，如此貼近人生，道盡了愛情的無可奈何，激起讀者心靈的微波，久久低迴不已。

水啊，水啊，
到處都是水

◆ 柯爾律治 Samuel Taylor Coleridge

CD*21

Water, water everywhere,

Nor any drop to drink.

水啊，水啊，到處都是水，

卻沒有一滴能解我乾渴。

這段詩出自英國詩人柯爾律治的長詩〈古舟子詠〉（The Rime of the Ancient Mariner）。

全詩瀰漫著迷茫徜恍，縹渺幽微的意緒。〈古舟子詠〉視爲詩人自己的人生之夢，老水手即柯爾律治本人，老水手的苦難象徵著詩人的掙扎，最後在入港時終得解脫。詩中滿是哥德式故事的恐懼，恍兮惚兮的神話：「冰雪在怒吼，冰雪在咆哮／像人昏厥時聽到的隆隆巨響。」直到水手發現，周遭環繞著鹹鹹的汪洋大海，水啊，水啊，到處都是水，卻沒有一滴水能入口，船員來不及呻吟嘆息，在星月下一個個倒斃。

這段詩常常引用於雖然夠多，但卻一個也沒辦法用的情況下。

我的老美同學曾經開玩笑，改寫了這段詩：

Women, women everywhere,
Nor any one to love.

唐朝詩人溫飛卿有句詩，
意境類同：

「過盡千帆皆不是，
斜暉脈脈水悠悠。」

電視影集《慾望城市》第四季第16集，凱莉當時手頭很緊，一向喜歡買名牌高跟鞋的她，這日走入鞋店，看到架上一雙又一雙漂亮的鞋子，心裡雖想卻買不下手。於是感嘆道：

Water, water everywhere,
Not a drop to drink.

老虎
The Tiger

◆ 布雷克 William Blake

CD*22

布雷克
William Blake
（1757-1827）

英國詩人、畫家、雕版家。人稱「神祕主義詩人」，著有詩集《天真與經驗之歌》、散文集《天堂與地獄的婚姻》。

Tiger, tiger, burning bright
In the forest of the night,
What immortal hand or eye
Could frame thy fearful symmetry?

老虎！老虎！火一樣輝煌，
燃燒在那深夜的叢莽。
是什麼超凡的手和眼睛
塑造出你這可怖的勻稱？

美國電視影集《熱血警探》（*Touching Evil*）在播放一季之後，短命結束了。

這齣影集改編自英國熱門電視劇，傑夫瑞·唐納文（Jeffrey Donovan）在劇中飾演擁有神奇第六感，卻又有厭世傾向的刑事警官。一次槍擊案，造成他「死」了十分鐘，又活了過來，但已神智不清，住進精神病院一陣子。

他復原後又回到警局服務，有一回，他與另一女警搭飛機前往丹佛辦案。在飛機上，他說著說著，對現世充滿憤慨，情緒激昂，全身熱血沸騰，布雷克的詩句就這樣從他口中，悠悠而出：「老虎，老虎！」

布雷克能詩能畫，〈老虎！〉一詩表現出一種驚詫的強烈感覺。詩裡以上帝比喻猛虎；而猛虎的力氣如此有勁，身形如此壯美，氣勢又是如此奔放，使人聯想到它一定是上帝力排眾議，甘冒危險，施展神威的產物。

這首詩，不僅具有象徵意味，且含有預言的性質。詩人以斬截突兀、鏗鏘有力的節奏，有如錘鐵般的音調，塑造了「老虎」雄偉而可怖的形象，可能象徵革命的暴力，預示著震天撼地的力量。

美即是眞，眞即是美

◆ 濟慈 John Keats
CD*23

濟慈
John Keats（1795-1821）

英國十九世紀浪漫詩人，和拜倫、雪萊並稱於世。1921年死於肺病，年僅26。

"Beauty is truth, truth beauty, —that is all
Ye know on earth, and all ye need to know."

「美即是眞，眞即是美，——這就包括
你們所知道、和該知道的一切。」

濟慈

柏拉圖曾經說過，美可帶我們走向眞理，至終，美和眞將合而爲一。濟慈（1795-1821）在〈希臘古甕頌〉（Ode on a Grecian Urn）一詩的最後兩行道出此一信念。

詩人一開始就把古甕擬人化了，花瓶不只是花瓶，而是一個觀照：「在你的形體上，豈非繚繞著古老的傳說。」

詩人仔細地端詳整個花瓶，雕工的精細。濟慈在詩中所讚美的對象是一只希臘古甕上描繪的情景：綠蔭下，俊美的小伙子熱烈追求含羞而躲避的少女，透過濟慈的名詩而流傳後世。在細緻揣摩中，詩人已經忘卻了花瓶的存在，漸漸地與瓶身上的畫面故事角色融爲一體，詩可以說比那甕上的畫更生動，更具韻味。

一如萊辛所言：「畫家只能暗示動態……但在詩裡，卻保持它的本色，它是一種稍縱即逝且百看不厭的美。」在詩裡，想像中的一切比現實要美得多，沒有聽見的音樂更美。

可惜我不能同時
走兩條路

◆ 佛洛斯特 Robert Frost
CD*23

佛洛斯特
Robert Frost（1874-1963）

美國詩人。早年，佛洛斯特的
詩在美國沒有受到重視，直到
在英國成名，他才返鄉。1961
年受邀在甘迺迪總統就職典裡
上朗讀〈全心的奉獻〉一詩。

Two roads diverged in a yellow wood,
And sorry I could not travel both.

黃樹林中有兩條路，
可惜我不能兩條都走。

這段詩引自美國詩人佛洛斯特的詩〈未竟之路〉（The Road not Taken）。

美國電視影集《CSI：犯罪現場》（*CSI: Crime Scene Investigation*），劇情背景在賭城拉斯維加斯。每當有凶殺案發生，CSI派調查員到現場勘察，採集犯罪線索，鎖定嫌疑犯，再由警方逮捕凶手到案。

其中一集，由於案子撲朔迷離，現場附近一時搜尋不著任何線索，尤其是被害人所搭的那條小船，竟然消失無蹤。這怎麼可能，一條小船就這樣蒸發了？

在苦思不得其果之下，男調查員於是在實驗室裡以科學方法作實驗求證，而女調查員則採腳踏實地方式，沿著犯罪現場的湖邊一路追蹤，不錯過任何蛛絲馬跡，終於在密密草叢深處發現了那條船。

看樣子，女調查員略勝一著。然而，作實驗求證也有其必要。但一個人又不能同時進行兩件事。

男調查員有感而發對年輕屬下說："Sorry, I could not travel both."（可惜我不能同時走兩條路）。

小伙子一聽就明白，立刻回答："Robert Frost's poem."（佛洛斯特的詩）

佛洛斯特

較少人走的路

◆ 佛洛斯特 Robert Frost
CD*23

Two roads diverged in a wood, and I—
I took the one less traveled by,
And that has made all the difference.

樹林中有兩條路，
而我選了那條較少人走的路，
這就造成了所有的差異。

佛洛斯特

如果給你一個機會重新選擇，你會追求絢爛還是歸於平淡？唸藝術或學理工，你會選擇哪一行？電影《扭轉奇蹟》（The Family Man）說的是一個聖誕夜的奇蹟，也是一個夢想和幸福的追尋。

十三年前，傑克‧坎貝爾（尼可拉斯‧凱吉飾）未履行對女友凱特（蒂‧李歐妮飾）的承諾，兩人各自分飛。而今，傑克已是個高薪又有權勢的單身漢，在華爾街過著名流仕紳的生活。直到有一天，舊日女友打電話來，勾起了當年的回憶——想當初，他差點兒娶了她……

一旁的女助理聽了，以為又是一段令人掉淚的傷心故事。傑克頓了頓，卻道：

「我選擇較少人走的路。」（I took the road less traveled.）

哪條路才是較多人走的呢？依世俗標準，傑克當年若娶凱特為妻，十三年後的今天，他應該已有一雙兒女，又因為要照顧家庭，他可能無法每天工作十八個鐘頭，爬到今天CEO的位置，而且他也可能從事別的行業，不在多金的華爾街……

這句話引自美國詩人佛洛斯特的詩〈未竟之路〉（The Road not Taken），曾獲選為2000年全美最受歡迎的一首詩。有唸過高中的美國人都能朗朗上口。

傑克在電影中有機會重新選擇，於是，他挑了另一條路：一夕之間從CEO變成居家男人，住的房子也從紐約豪華公寓變成紐澤西的尋常住宅。電影的劇情可由導演和編劇任意安排，但我們自己的人生呢？有時上了這條路，你以為可以隨時回頭換走另一條，現實則不然，一如佛洛斯特的詩。

每一位讀者都能在這首詩中結合自己的人生體驗，理解其中的哲理。因為人生就是不斷的做選擇，而選擇必然產生差異，幸與不幸，快樂與悲哀，希望和失望，究竟哪一條路才是最佳的路，眼前很難說。要等到日子久了，一切才顯出差異，但若想再回頭，已遲。

佛洛斯特

佛洛斯特的那道石牆

電影：《刺激1995》（*The Shawshank Redemption*）

電影裡的字眼：a Robert Frost poem

　　由恐怖大師史蒂芬‧金（Stephen King）的一篇並不恐怖的短篇小說改編的電影《刺激1995》。全片闡述人性的善與惡，活著就是因為有「希望」（hope），無罪的人堅忍到底，最後終得解脫，重獲自由。

　　銀行家安迪‧杜弗倫（提姆‧羅賓斯飾）坐了19年的冤獄，長期忍耐，只為了有一天能走出去。在逃獄前，他向獄中的患難之交瑞德（摩根‧費里曼飾）交待：

　　將來你假釋後，幫我個忙，在巴克斯頓（緬因州）有一片牧草田。答應我，瑞德，只要你出得去，找到那地方。

　　瑞德沒有聽明白，他說巴克斯頓那一帶的田很多。

　　「有一處不同，它有長長的石牆，北端有棵大橡樹，就像佛洛斯特的一首詩。」（One in particular. Got a long rock wall with a big oak at the north end. Like something out of a Robert Frost poem.）

　　四度普利茲獎得主佛洛斯特的一首詩，指的是＜補牆＞（Mending Wall）。我在新罕布夏州佛洛斯特故居親眼見到他描寫的那道石牆。

　　這是美國新英格蘭區（包括緬因、新罕布夏、佛蒙特、康乃迪克及麻州）特有的石牆，用當地石頭像堆積木似的一塊塊堆壘成一片牆，沒有用任何外物加固，可以隨時搬開拆牆，常用來區隔兩家之間的田地。

　　本片背景在緬因州。安迪要瑞德到石牆底下，有一塊火山石，底下埋著東西給他，只要把石頭搬開就會看到。

　　「好籬笆維持好鄰居」（Good fences make good neighbors.）

　　意指人與人之間應該保持適當的距離，以免過度親密易生侮慢之心。這句詩出現在休葛蘭主演的《求婚腦震盪》（*Mickey Blue Eyes*）電影中。

佛洛斯特

去奮鬥，去追尋，
去發現，永不放棄

◆丁尼生 Alfred, Lord Tennyson

CD*23

丁尼生
Alfred Lord Tennyson
（1809-1892）

英國詩人。1828年就讀
劍橋大學時，高大英俊
的他已頗有詩名。在維
多利亞時代，他繼華滋
華斯之後當了四十餘年
桂冠詩人。

To strive, to seek, to find, and not to yield.

去奮鬥，去追尋，去發現，永不放棄。

丁尼生

一天，我去拜訪一個律師朋友，在辦公室裡，他的案頭上擺了一塊區牌，上面寫道："To strive, to seek, to find, and not to yield."（去奮鬥，去追求，去發現，永不放棄。）

英國桂冠詩人丁尼生在他的詩作〈尤利西斯〉（Ulysses）中，想像自己年華已老，又因長年海上生活而疲憊憔悴，這時他思索著，在走遍全世界之後，如果人生能夠重來，他會有什麼樣的選擇呢？

「縱然失去許多，也留下許多；縱然不再年輕力壯，氣壯山河，然而我們依舊是我們；英雄的心靈，因時光的流逝，命運的摧殘而奄奄一息。不變的是剛強的意志，去奮鬥，去追求，去發現，永不放棄。」（Tho' much is taken, much abides; and tho' / We are not now that strength which in the old days / Moved earth and heaven; that which we are, we are;/ One equal-temper of heroic hearts,/ Made weak by time and fate, but strong in will/ To strive, to seek, to find, and not to yield. ）

一首詩，在不同的年齡閱讀，所得的感觸也不一樣。香港前政務司長陳方安生曾經說：受人生經驗的影響，她直至退休前七年，才領悟英國詩人丁尼生詩作〈尤利西斯〉的「詩意」。說到生命的意義，「那美好的仗我已經打過了，該跑的路我已經跑盡了。」這位香港人口中的「陳太」在退休之際，她引用了一句丁尼生的詩獻給香港市民：「我們的人生應該是『去奮鬥，去追求，去發現，永不放棄。』」

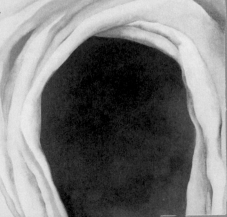

愛過總比沒愛好

◆丁尼生 Alfred, Lord Tennyson

CD*23

'Tis better to have loved and lost
Than never to have loved at all.

寧願愛過而又失去，
總比從未愛過好。

你曾經傷過心嗎？而今，你依然落淚嗎？

　　因爲他忘了今天是七夕，或者，他早已經把你給忘記。

　　你給他傳了e-mail，你給他傳了簡訊，甚至你故意找了藉口打電話給他。輕描淡寫說一聲：「祝你七夕情人節快樂！」

　　他——冷漠以待。

　　你以爲相別離是多麼傷痛的事，你以爲淚水即將流盡。

　　要慶幸啊，因爲你還有心，所以你會痛；因爲你是個有感情的人，所以你會流淚。

　　其實，你失去了的，有時不是愛，而是那份可笑的自尊或尊嚴。

　　然而要記住，永遠都有更好的人在前面等著你，你要耐心等待。拐個彎，感情就有新的出口；對愛的憧憬，值得你去把握。

　　不要再折磨自己，要讓自己過得更好。

　　你要勇敢尋找屬於你的眞愛，但不要輕易給予你的愛。

　　今夜是七夕，願天下有情人，有緣相聚。在此，給曾經愛過又傷了心的你：

　　寧願愛過而又失去，

　　總比從未愛過好。

附注：

'tis 是it is 的縮寫。

這句詩出自丁尼生的〈悼念集〉（In Memoriam AHH），把131首抒情短詩串在一起的長詩。爲了悼念同學哈勒姆而作，詩句卻遠遠超出了悼念的範圍。詩人不僅是發抒悼友之情，追念彼此的友誼，而且還以「天問」的姿態反映了一個時代的信仰危機和痛苦思索。

丁尼生

大詩人的聲音

騎兵旅的衝鋒

The Charge of the Light Brigade

◆丁尼生 Alfred, Lord Tennyson

朗誦：丁尼生

（CD*24，自第1-3段*處）

*Half a league, half a league,
Half a league onward,
All in the valley of Death
Rode the six hundred.
"Forward, the Light Brigade!
"Charge for the guns!" he said:
Into the valley of Death
Rode the six hundred.

* "Forward, the Light Brigade!"
Was there a man dismay'd?
Not tho' the soldier knew
Someone had blunder'd:
Their's not to make reply,
Their's not to reason why,
Their's but to do and die:
Into the valley of Death
Rode the six hundred.

半數盟軍，半數盟軍，
半數盟軍前進，
全在死亡之谷
六百驃騎向前。
「前進，騎兵旅！
向火炮衝鋒！」他說：
進入死亡之谷
六百驃騎向前。

「前進，騎兵旅！」
難道有人灰心？
沒有，雖然戰士知道
有人疏忽犯錯：
他們沒有回答，
他們不問原因，
只是去戰去死：
進入死亡之谷
六百驃騎向前。

*Cannon to right of them,
Cannon to left of them,
Cannon in front of them
Volley'd and thunder'd;
Storm'd at with shot and shell,
Boldly they rode and well,
Into the jaws of Death,
Into the mouth of Hell
Rode the six hundred.

大炮在他們右邊，
大炮在他們左邊，
大炮在他們前面
萬彈齊發炸雷轟天；
槍炮猛擊猶如暴雨，
他們英勇無畏策馬飛身，
進入鬼門關，
進入地獄之口
六百驃騎向前。

Flash'd all their sabres bare,
Flash'd as they turn'd in air,
Sabring the gunners there,
Charging an army, while
All the world wonder'd:
Plunged in the battery-smoke
Right thro' the line they broke;
Cossack and Russian
Reel'd from the sabre stroke
Shatter'd and sunder'd.
Then they rode back, but not
Not the six hundred.

他們所有的軍刀出鞘閃閃發光，
空中揮舞寒光閃閃，
砍殺那裡的槍砲手，
砍殺敵人，而
全世界都為之驚歎：
衝入炮火硝煙
直搗敵陣前鋒；
哥薩克和俄羅斯兵
從白刃戰退縮
潰垮離散。
然後他們騎返，但不再
是六百驃騎壯漢。

Cannon to right of them,
Cannon to left of them,
Cannon behind them
Volley'd and thunder'd;
Storm'd at with shot and shell,
While horse and hero fell,
They that had fought so well
Came thro' the jaws of Death
Back from the mouth of Hell,
All that was left of them,
Left of six hundred.

大炮在他們右邊，
大炮在他們左邊，
大炮在他們前面
萬彈齊發炸雷轟天；
槍炮猛擊猶如暴雨，
儘管戰馬和英雄倒下去了，
他們已打過如此漂亮的激戰，
穿過鬼門關
從地獄之口回返，
所有他們存活的，
六百驃騎好漢中存活的。

When can their glory fade?
O the wild charge they made!
All the world wondered.
Honor the charge they made,
Honor the Light Brigade,
Noble six hundred.

他們的榮耀何時會褪色？
啊，他們打過最激烈的衝鋒！
全世界都爲之驚歎。
榮譽歸於他們的衝鋒，
榮譽歸於騎兵旅，
傑出的六百驃騎英雄。

丁尼生

家，甜蜜的家
Home, Sweet Home

◆ 約翰‧佩恩 John H. Payne
CD*25

Home, Home, sweet, sweet Home!
There's no place like Home! There's no place like Home!

家啊！家啊！甜蜜的家！
沒有地方比得上家！沒有地方比得上家！

這段詩句出現在電影《綠野仙蹤》（*The Wizard of Oz*）的尾聲。

　　這部著名的美國經典童話，含意深遠，對兒童也極具教育意義。美國中西部平原上的小女孩桃樂絲被一陣龍捲風吹到陌生的國度，她遇見稻草人、錫樵夫、膽小獅，一行人沿著黃磚道前往奧茲國，向偉大的魔法師祈求完成個人的心願——

　　桃樂絲想知道回家的路；稻草人想要換新腦袋；膽小獅想要有勇氣；錫樵夫則想要有一顆心……大家都以為只要找到了魔法師，再難的問題都能夠解決。幾經波折，歷經萬險，好不容易來到奧茲國，他們一不小心揭開了「魔法師」的神祕面紗，原來他不過是一個普通老頭子。

　　但這時候，魔法師也點醒了這一行人，說稻草人能想方設法，表示他有腦袋；錫樵夫心地善良，證明他本來就有心；而膽小獅勇敢幫助眾人，意謂著他有勇氣；至於桃樂絲呢？回家的方法就在她自己的腳上。當她終於回到堪薩斯，回到那簡樸的農村家庭，她終於發現，原來世上沒有任何地方，比得上自己的家好。

"There's no place like home!"

也有人翻譯：「金窩、銀窩，不如自己的狗窩。」

約翰・佩恩

少即是多

◆ 白朗寧 Robert Browning
CD*25

白朗寧
Robert Browning
（1812-1889）

英國詩人，最受歡迎的
詩集有《戲劇抒情詩》、
《戲劇羅曼史和抒情
詩》、《男男女女》、
《劇中人物》等，其中包
括描寫眾生百態的戲劇
獨白詩。他的妻子白朗
寧夫人（Elizabeth
Browning）也是著名的
詩人。

Less is more.

少即是多。

大詩人的聲音

成寒詩話

二十世紀建築四大師之一，路德威‧密斯‧凡德羅（Ludwig Mies van der Rohe, 1886-1969）的名言：「簡潔就是豐富」，又譯：「少即是多」，這句話成了建築設計人常喊的口號。

從1930年至1933年，密斯繼創辦人葛羅培斯（Walter Gropius）領導包浩斯的最後時期，並從德紹（Dessau）遷至柏林，後移民美國。他強調好的現代建築，不得有形式，一切從零開始，就這樣「零即是無限」、「少即是多」的哲學，從他的建築嚴謹而簡潔的外表可得到印證。

然而，大家都把「少即是多」歸於密斯的創意，我要在此提出申訴，這句話實際上是出自詩人白朗寧1855年的詩作〈Andrea del Sarto, 1. 78, *Men and Women*, vol. 2〉。

他們如何從根特帶好消息到艾克斯

How They Brought the Good News from Ghent to Aix

◆ 白朗寧 Robert Browning

I sprang to the stirrup, and Joris, and he;
I galloped, Dirck galloped, we galloped all three;
"Good speed!" cried the watch, as the gate-bolts undrew;
"Speed!" echoed the wall to us galloping through;
Behind shut the postern, the lights sank to rest,
And into the midnight we galloped abreast.

Not a word to each other; we kept the great pace
Neck by neck, stride by stride, never changing our place;
I turned in my saddle and made its girths tight,
Then shortened each stirrup, and set the pique right,
Rebuckled the cheek-strap, chained slacker the bit,
Nor galloped less steadily Roland a whit.

成寒詩話

白朗寧（1812-1889）錄這首詩年已近八十，因爲從來沒見過留聲機，錄音時有點亢奮激動，唸到最後自己大聲叫好，還拍手鼓掌。

由於年代久遠及當時的錄音技術欠佳，本詩聽起來並不十分清晰。但此錄音有彌足珍貴之價值。

附注：詩中的兩個人名：Joris & Dirck 是荷蘭文，相等於英文名字：George & Derrick。

附錄

假如我告訴他：
畢卡索的完整描述

If I Told Him: A Completed Portrait of Picasso

◆ 葛楚・史坦 Gertrude Stein
朗讀：葛楚・史坦
CD*26

葛楚・史坦
Gertrude Stein（1874-1946）

美國作家及詩人。她長居巴黎多年，結交當代作家及畫家如海明威、畢卡索等人，她說海明威這些人都是「失落的一代」（Lost Generation）。

圖為〈葛楚・史坦〉，畢卡索繪。

If I told him would he like it. Would he like it if I
told him.
Would he like it would Napoleon would Napoleon
would would he like it.
If Napoleon if I told him if I told him if Napoleon.
Would he like it if I told him if I told him if
Napoleon. Would he like it if Napoleon if Napoleon
if I told him. If I told him if Napoleon if Napoleon
if I told him. If I told him would he
like it would he like it if I told him.
Now.
Not now.
And now.
Now.
Exactly as as kings.
Feeling full for it.
Exactitude as kings.
So to beseech you as full as for it.
Exactly or as kings.
Shutters shut and open so do queens. Shutters shut and shutters and so shutters shut

and shutters and so and so shutters and so shutters shut and so shutters shut and shutters and so. And so shutters shut and so and also. And also and so and so and also. Exact resemblance. To exact resemblance the exact resemblance as exact as a resemblance, exactly as resembling, exactly resembling, exactly in resemblance exactly a resemblance, exactly and resemblance. For this is so. Because.

Now actively repeat at all, now actively repeat at all, now actively repeat at all.

Have hold and hear, actively repeat at all.

I judge judge.

As a resemblance to him.

Who comes first. Napoleon the first.

Who comes too coming coming too, who goes there, as they go they share, who shares all, all is as all as as yet or as yet.

Now to date now to date. Now and now and date and the date.

Who came first. Napoleon at first. Who came first Napoleon the first.

Who came first, Napoleon first.

Presently.

Exactly do they do.

First exactly.

Exactly do they do too.

First exactly.

And first exactly.

Exactly do they do.

And first exactly and exactly.

And do they do.

At first exactly and first exactly and do they do.

The first exactly.

And do they do.

The first exactly.

At first exactly.

First as exactly.

As first as exactly.

Presently

As presently.

As as presently.

He he he he and he and he and and he and he and he and and as and as he and as he and he. He is and as he is, and as he is and he is, he is and as he and he and as he is and he and he and and he and he.

Can curls rob can curls quote, quotable.

As presently.

As exactitude.

As trains

Has trains.

Has trains.

As trains.

As trains.

Presently.

Proportions.

Presently.

As proportions as presently.

Father and farther.

Was the king or room.

Farther and whether.

Was there was there was there what was there was there what was there was there there was there.

Whether and in there.

As even say so.

One.

I land.

Two.

I land.

Three.

The land.

Three

The land.

Three

The land.

Two

I land.

Two

I land.

One

I land.

Two

I land.

As a so.

They cannot.

A note.

They cannot.

A float.

They cannot.

They dote.

They cannot.

They as denote.

Miracles play.

Play fairly.

Play fairly well.

A well.

As well.

As or as presently.

Let me recite what history teaches. History teaches.

圖爲〈畢卡索肖像〉，畢卡索繪。

1920年代的巴黎，許多美國人，尤其是文人和藝術家紛紛跑到巴黎去生活，比如說詩人龐德、福特、小說家海明威、費滋傑羅、葛楚・史坦等人，外界稱他們是「流亡人士」或「放逐人士」（expatriate），從自己的國家流浪到他鄉。這些人在巴黎發生了許多故事，而他們筆下的許多文學作品都是以巴黎爲背景，如海明威《旭日又東升》（*The Sun Also Rises*）以及海明威晚年寫的，紀錄1921年至1926年他和第一任妻子在巴黎的那段歲月《流動的饗宴》（*A Moveable Feast*）。

葛楚・史坦是典型的「美國人在巴黎」，她以貴族氣質彩繪其詩篇，朗誦時微微帶點英國腔。葛楚・史坦來到巴黎以後結識許多藝文人士，她很幸運，有機會讓在畫壇剛起了聲名的畢卡索繪了一幅畫像，從此就跟著大畫家一起永垂不朽。

一個孩童在威爾斯的聖誕節
A Child's Christmas in Wales

朗讀：Dylan Thomas
CD*27

One Christmas was so much like another, in those years around the sea-town corner now and out of all sound except the distant speaking of the voices I sometimes hear a moment before sleep, that I can never remember whether it snowed for six days and six nights when I was twelve or whether it snowed for twelve days and twelve nights when I was six.

All the Christmases roll down toward the two-tongued sea, like a cold and headlong moon bundling down the sky that was our street; and they stop at the rim of the ice-edged fish-freezing waves, and I plunge my hands in the snow and bring out whatever I can find. In goes my hand into that wool-white bell-tongued ball of holidays resting at the rim of the carol-singing sea, and out come Mrs. Prothero and the firemen.

It was on the afternoon of the Christmas Eve, and I was in Mrs. Prothero's garden, waiting for cats, with her son Jim. It was snowing. It was always snowing at Christmas. December, in my memory, is white as Lapland, though there were no reindeers. But there were cats. Patient, cold and callous, our hands wrapped in socks, we waited to snowball the cats. Sleek and long as jaguars and horrible-whiskered, spitting and snarling, they would slink and sidle over the white back-garden walls, and the lynx-eyed hunters, Jim and I, fur-capped and moccasined trappers from Hudson Bay, off Mumbles Road, would hurl our deadly snowballs at the green of their eyes. The wise cats never appeared.

We were so still, Eskimo-footed arctic marksmen in the muffling silence of the eternal snows——eternal, ever since Wednesday——that we never heard Mrs. Prothero's first cry from her igloo at the bottom of the garden. Or, if we heard it at all, it was, to us, like the far-off challenge of our enemy and prey, the neighbor's polar cat. But soon the voice grew louder.

"Fire!" cried Mrs. Prothero, and she beat the dinner-gong.

And we ran down the garden, with the snowballs in our arms, toward the house; and smoke, indeed, was pouring out of the dining-room, and the gong was bombilating, and Mrs. Prothero was announcing ruin like a town crier in Pompeii. This was better than all the cats in Wales standing on the wall in a row. We bounded into the house, laden with snowballs, and stopped at the open door of the smoke-filled room.

Something was burning all right; perhaps it was Mr. Prothero, who always slept there after midday dinner with a newspaper over his face. But he was standing in the middle of the room, saying, "A fine Christmas!" and smacking at the smoke with a slipper.

"Call the fire brigade," cried Mrs. Prothero as she beat the gong.

"There won't be here," said Mr. Prothero, "it's Christmas."

There was no fire to be seen, only clouds of smoke and Mr. Prothero standing in the middle of them, waving his slipper as though he were conducting.

"Do something," he said. And we threw all our snowballs into the smoke——I think we missed Mr. Prothero——and ran out of the house to the telephone box.

"Let's call the police as well," Jim said. "And the ambulance." "And Ernie Jenkins, he likes fires."

But we only called the fire brigade, and soon the fire engine came and three tall men in helmets brought a hose into the house and Mr. Prothero got out just in time before they turned it on. Nobody could have had a noisier Christmas Eve. And when the firemen turned off the hose and were standing in the wet, smoky room,

Jim's Aunt, Miss. Prothero, came downstairs and peered in at them. Jim and I waited, very quietly, to hear what she would say to them. She said the right thing, always. She looked at the three tall firemen in their shining helmets, standing among the smoke and cinders and dissolving snowballs, and she said, "Would you like anything to read?"

Years and years ago, when I was a boy, when there were wolves in Wales, and birds the color of red-flannel petticoats whisked past the harp-shaped hills, when we sang and wallowed all night and day in caves that smelt like Sunday afternoons in damp front farmhouse parlors, and we chased, with the jawbones of deacons, the English and the bears, before the motor car, before the wheel, before the duchess-faced horse, when we rode the daft and happy hills bareback, it snowed and it snowed. But here a small boy says: "It snowed last year, too. I made a snowman and my brother knocked it down and I knocked my brother down and then we had tea."

"But that was not the same snow," I say. "Our snow was not only shaken from white wash buckets down the sky, it came shawling out of the ground and swam and drifted out of the arms and hands and bodies of the trees; snow grew overnight on the roofs of the houses like a pure and grandfather moss, minutely——ivied the walls and settled on the postman, opening the gate, like a dumb, numb thunderstorm of white, torn Christmas cards."

"Were there postmen then, too?"

"With sprinkling eyes and wind-cherried noses, on spread, frozen feet they crunched up to the doors and mittened on them manfully. But all that the children could hear was a ringing of bells."

"You mean that the postman went rat-a-tat-tat and the doors rang?"

"I mean that the bells the children could hear were inside them."

"I only hear thunder sometimes, never bells."

"There were church bells, too."

"Inside them?"

"No, no, no, in the bat-black, snow-white belfries, tugged by bishops and storks. And they rang their tidings over the bandaged town, over the frozen foam of the powder and ice-cream hills, over the crackling sea. It seemed that all the churches boomed for joy under my window; and the weathercocks crew for Christmas, on our fence."

"Get back to the postmen."

"They were just ordinary postmen, found of walking and dogs and Christmas and the snow. They knocked on the doors with blue knuckles..."

"Ours has got a black knocker..."

"And then they stood on the white Welcome mat in the little, drifted porches and huffed and puffed, making ghosts with their breath, and jogged from foot to foot like small boys wanting to go out."

"And then the presents?"

"And then the Presents, after the Christmas box. And the cold postman, with a rose on his button-nose, tingled down the tea-tray-slithered run of the chilly glinting hill. He went in his ice-bound boots like a man on fishmonger's slabs."

"He wagged his bag like a frozen camel's hump, dizzily turned the corner on one foot, and, by God, he was gone."

"Get back to the Presents."

"There were the Useful Presents: engulfing mufflers of the old coach days, and mittens made for giant sloths; zebra scarfs of a substance like silky gum that could be tug-o'-warred down to the galoshes; blinding tam-o'-shanters like patchwork tea cozies and bunny-suited busbies and balaclavas for victims of head-shrinking tribes; from aunts who always wore wool next to the skin there were mustached and rasping vests that made you wonder why the aunts had any skin left at all; and once I had a little crocheted nose bag from an aunt now, alas, no longer whinnying with us. And pictureless books in which small boys, though warned with quotations not to, would skate on Farmer Giles' pond and did and drowned; and books that told me everything about the wasp, except why."

"Go on the Useless Presents."

"Bags of moist and many-colored jelly babies and a folded flag and a false nose and a tram-conductor's cap and a machine that punched tickets and rang a bell; never a catapult; once, by mistake that no one could explain, a little hatchet; and a celluloid duck that made, when you pressed it, a most unducklike sound, a mewing moo that an ambitious cat might make who wished to be a cow; and a painting book in which I could make the grass, the trees, the sea and the animals any colour I pleased, and still the dazzling sky-blue sheep are grazing in the red field under the rainbow-billed and pea-green birds. Hardboileds, toffee, fudge and allsorts, crunches, cracknels, humbugs, glaciers, marzipan, and butterwelsh for the Welsh. And troops of bright tin soldiers who, if they could not fight, could always run. And Snakes-and-Families and Happy Ladders. And Easy Hobbi-Games for Little Engineers, complete with instructions. Oh, easy for Leonardo! And a whistle to make the dogs bark to wake up the old man next door to make him beat on the wall with his stick to shake our picture off the wall. And a packet of cigarettes: you put one in your mouth and you stood at the corner of the street and you waited for hours, in vain, for an old lady to scold you for smoking a cigarette, and then with a smirk you ate it. And then it was breakfast under the balloons."

"Were there Uncles like in our house?"

"There are always Uncles at Christmas. The same Uncles. And on Christmas morning, with dog-disturbing whistle and sugar fags, I would scour the swatched town for the news of the little world, and find always a dead bird by the Post Office or by the white deserted swings; perhaps a robin, all but one of his fires out. Men and women wading or scooping back from chapel, with taproom noses and wind-bussed cheeks, all albinos, huddles their stiff black jarring feathers against the irre-ligious snow. Mistletoe hung from the gas brackets in all the front parlors; there was sherry and walnuts and bottled beer and crackers by the dessertspoons; and cats in their fur-abouts watched the fires; and the high-heaped fire spat, all ready for the chestnuts and the mulling pokers. Some few large men sat in the front parlors, without their collars, Uncles almost certainly, trying their new cigars, holding them out judiciously at arms' length, returning them to their mouths, coughing, then holding them out again as though waiting for the explosion; and some few small aunts, not wanted in the kitchen, nor anywhere else for that matter, sat on the very edge of their chairs, poised and brittle, afraid to break, like faded cups and saucers."

Not many those mornings trod the piling streets: an old man always, fawn-bowlered, yellow-gloved and, at this time of year, with spats of snow, would take his constitutional to the white bowling green and back, as he would take it wet or fire on Christmas Day or Doomsday; sometimes two hale young men, with big pipes blazing, no overcoats and wind blown scarfs, would trudge, unspeaking, down to the forlorn sea, to work up an appetite, to blow away the fumes, who knows, to walk into the waves until nothing of them was left but the two furling smoke clouds of their inextinguishable briars. Then I would be slap-dashing home, the gravy smell of the dinners of others, the bird smell, the brandy, the pudding and mince, coiling up to my nostrils, when out of a snow-clogged side lane would come a boy the spit of myself, with a pink-tipped cigarette and the violet past of a black eye, cocky as a bullfinch, leering all to himself.

I hated him on sight and sound, and would be about to put my dog whistle to my lips and blow him off the face of Christmas when suddenly he, with a violet wink, put his whistle to his lips and blew so stridently, so high, so exquisitely loud, that gobbling faces, their cheeks bulged with goose, would press against their tinsled windows, the whole length of the white echoing street. For dinner we had turkey and blazing pudding, and after dinner the Uncles sat in front of the fire, loosened all buttons, put their large moist hands over their watch chains, groaned a little and slept. Mothers, aunts and sisters scuttled to and fro, bearing tureens. Auntie Bessie, who had already been frightened, twice, by a clock-work mouse, whimpered at the sideboard and had some elderberry wine. The dog was sick. Auntie Dosie had to have three aspirins, but Auntie Hannah, who liked port, stood in the middle of the snowbound back yard, singing like a big-bosomed thrush. I would blow up balloons to see how big they would blow up to; and, when they burst, which they all did, the Uncles jumped and rumbled. In the rich and heavy afternoon, the Uncles breathing like dolphins and the snow descending, I would sit among festoons and Chinese lanterns and nibble dates and try to make a model man-o'-war, following the Instructions for Little Engineers, and produce what might be mistaken for a sea-going tramcar.

Or I would go out, my bright new boots squeaking, into the white world, on to the seaward hill, to call on Jim and Dan and Jack and to pad through the still streets, leaving huge deep footprints on the hidden pavements.

"I bet people will think there's been hippos."

"What would you do if you saw a hippo coming down our street?"

"I'd go like this, bang! I'd throw him over the railings and roll him down the hill and then I'd tickle him under the ear and he'd wag his tail."

"What would you do if you saw two hippos?"

Iron-flanked and bellowing he-hippos clanked and battered through the scudding snow toward us as we passed Mr. Daniel's house.

"Let's post Mr. Daniel a snow-ball through his letter box."

"Let's write things in the snow."

"Let's write, 'Mr. Daniel looks like a spaniel' all over his lawn."

Or we walked on the white shore. "Can the fishes see it's snowing?"

The silent one-clouded heavens drifted on to the sea. Now we were snow-blind travelers lost on the north hills, and vast dewlapped dogs, with flasks round their necks, ambled and shambled up to us, baying "Excelsior." We returned home through the poor streets where only a few children fumbled with bare red fingers in the wheel-rutted snow and cat-called after us, their voices fading away, as we trudged uphill, into the cries of the dock birds and the hooting of ships out in the whirling bay. And then, at tea the recovered Uncles would be jolly; and the ice cake loomed in the center of the table like a marble grave. Auntie Hannah laced her tea with rum, because it was only once a year.

Bring out the tall tales now that we told by the fire as the gaslight bubbled like a diver. Ghosts whooed like owls in the long nights when I dared not look over my shoulder; animals lurked in the cubbyhole under the stairs and the gas meter ticked. And I remember that we went singing carols once, when there wasn't the shaving of a moon to light the flying streets. At the end of a long road was a drive that led to a large house, and we stumbled up the darkness of the drive that night, each one of us afraid, each one holding a stone in his hand in case, and all of us too brave to say a word. The wind through the trees made noises as of old and unpleasant and maybe webfooted men wheezing in caves. We reached the black bulk of the house. "What shall we give them? Hark the Herald?"

"No," Jack said, "Good King Wencelas. I'll count three." One, two three, and we began to sing, our voices high and seemingly distant in the snow-felted dark-ness round the house that was occupied by nobody we knew. We stood close together, near the dark door. Good King Wencelas looked out On the Feast of Stephen ... And then a small, dry voice, like the voice of someone who has not spo-ken for a long time, joined our singing: a small, dry, eggshell voice from the other side of the door: a small dry voice through the keyhole. And when we stopped run-ning we were outside our house; the front room was lovely; balloons floated under the hot-water-bottle-gulping gas; everything was good again and shone over the town.

"Perhaps it was a ghost," Jim said.

"Perhaps it was trolls," Dan said, who was always reading.

"Let's go in and see if there's any jelly left," Jack said. And we did that.

Always on Christmas night there was music. An uncle played the fiddle, a cousin sang "Cherry Ripe," and another uncle sang "Drake's Drum." It was very warm in the little house. Auntie Hannah, who had got on to the parsnip wine, sang a song about Bleeding Hearts and Death, and then another in which she said her heart was like a Bird's Nest; and then everybody laughed again; and then I went to bed. Looking through my bedroom window, out into the moonlight and the unending smoke-colored snow, I could see the lights in the windows of all the other houses on our hill and hear the music rising from them up the long, steady falling night. I turned the gas down, I got into bed. I said some words to the close and holy darkness, and then I slept.

成寒品味系列1

大詩人的聲音

2004年11月初版　　　　　　　　　　　　　　　定價：新臺幣280元
2021年9月初版第十刷
有著作權・翻印必究
Printed in Taiwan.

編　著	成		寒
叢書主編	顏	艾	琳
	邱	靖	絨
校　對	楊	惠	君
封面設計	李	東	記

出　版　者	聯經出版事業股份有限公司	副總編輯	陳　逸　華
地　　　址	新北市汐止區大同路一段369號1樓	總編輯	涂　豐　恩
叢書主編電話	(02)86925588轉5305	總經理	陳　芝　宇
台北聯經書房	台北市新生南路三段94號	社　長	羅　國　俊
電　　　話	(02)23620308	發行人	林　載　爵
台中分公司	台中市北區崇德路一段198號		
暨門市電話	(04)22312023		
郵政劃撥帳戶	第0100559-3號		
郵撥電話	(02)23620308		
印　刷　者	文聯彩色製版印刷有限公司		
總　經　銷	聯合發行股份有限公司		
發　行　所	新北市新店區寶橋路235巷6弄6號2F		
電　　　話	(02)29178022		

行政院新聞局出版事業登記證局版臺業字第0130號

本書如有缺頁，破損，倒裝請寄回台北聯經書房更換。　ISBN　978-957-08-2783-5 (平裝附光碟)
聯經網址 http://www.linkingbooks.com.tw
電子信箱 e-mail:linking@udngroup.com

國家圖書館出版品預行編目資料

大詩人的聲音 / 成寒編著 . 初版 . 新北市 .
聯經 . 2004年 . 160面 . 16.5×21.5公分 .
（成寒品味系列；1）
ISBN　978-957-08-2783-5（平裝附光碟）
[2021年9月初版第十刷]

813.1　　　　　　　　　　　　　　93020473